The
Accidental Treasure
Hunters

Glyn Bryan

Dedication

To Jo and my sister Maggie in thanks for reading my manuscript and their suggestions for corrections and improvements

The Accidental Treasure Hunters

Imagine how a chance discovery whilst in France could lead an ordinary Oxfordshire couple into following a trail across the West Country and Wales in search of one of the greatest ancient treasures of all time. The history and the places are there for all to see but bringing the pieces together to solve the mystery brings with it an unexpected danger...

Contents

Chapter 1

In the early morning darkness of a chill October day in 1307, three heavily laden ships quietly slipped their moorings and headed down the Charente river from the French town of Angouleme towards the Bay of Biscay and the safety of the Atlantic ocean. The only sounds were of the water gently brushing their hulls and the occasional creak from the flexing of timbers or rigging. More importantly, the only witnesses to this departure were the sheep and cattle still dozing in pastures next to the quietly swirling river.

Aboard the first vessel stood a man in his late fifties; no longer in his physical prime perhaps but clearly someone who had been fit and strong in his younger days, someone who had the look and bearing of a man of authority. Philippe de Chretien wore the clothes of an ordinary farmer but he was in fact a Knight of the Templar Order. He was accompanied by his faithful squire Bernard who had been with him man and boy. Together they had explored the secrets of Jerusalem, battled with the Moors and survived near starvation on a journey to Constantinople. Now in the autumn of their lives they had once again been forced to take action in the face of danger.

The first sign of trouble was when Philippe had received an urgent message to collect a number of chests, boxes, barrels and sacks and get them far away from Paris as quickly and unobtrusively as possible. This was no mean feat and finding enough animals to carry all the loads had been a daunting task. Bernard had been under strict instructions to hire horses and men from only the most reliable and discrete sources. Suppliers had been paid handsomely but the whole process, followed by ten days of travel, had been exhausting.

While Bernard had been tasked with loading the contents of their train onto the ships, other caravans of horses, mules and oxen had been arriving from all over France each laden with more precious cargo to be taken onto the ships. Philippe had left Bernard in charge of the heaving, sweating throng and had gone to the house of a trusted friend of the Templars just a short distance up the hill from the quay. Here he had met with a fellow Templar who passed him a sealed scroll and whispered "this is direct from our Provincial Commander, Guillaume Hugolin, himself. He wishes you God's Blessing and God's speed." Philippe broke open the seal and studied the scroll contents carefully. He read it twice then screwed it into a ball and threw it onto the open fire.

Outside the bustle of loading had subsided and only the last few pieces remained to be packed away. The men in charge of the pack animals were paid off and, with a few embraces, handshakes and exchanges of wishes they disappeared back into the night.

Now on board the ship threading its way to the open sea, Bernard asked his Lord a question: "You have told me the Knights Templar will shortly be betrayed by our King and we must made good our escape from France, but why did we not go to La Rochelle instead of Angouleme, my Lord? It would have taken less time and do we not have our own ships in port there?" Philippe smiled and said "It is a matter of trust, my dear friend. The King's plans were revealed to us by a friend in his camp – but we cannot be certain that someone might not also betray our plans to his majesty. The whereabouts of our ships are known to many and it would have been a simple task for the King to spy on them and to have seized them once they had been laden with our wealth and the holy relics we are sworn to protect. By continuing further south any spies of the King might have thought we sought the protection of the English by heading for Gascony, but by the time they could have raised a force to intercept us we have already loaded our treasure onto ships and made good our departure."

Bernard smiled and nodded. Their past successes had often involved outwitting forces much stronger than their own and although they might no longer have the same strength and speed, it was clear the years had not dulled the Templar's strategic thinking. "So where do we go to now, my Lord?" asked Bernard. "We go to our old friend, Guy de Bryan, who I have not seen since our time together in the Crusades," replied Philippe. "We are going to the land of our Celtic brothers. It is well away from any spies of King Philip and we will have time and help to conceal our treasure from all our enemies." "Wales?" queried Bernard "but is the land safe for us there? Do not the Welsh fight against their Norman Lords?" "It is true the Welsh princes have not always been devoted to the King," agreed Philippe "but I am told that since King Edward returned from the Crusades and dealt with the Welsh the land has been at peace these 20 years since."

The little convoy sailed on, reaching the sea by dawn of the following day. They headed past Normandy and continued northwards across the open sea to the coast of Cornwall.

Chapter 2

It was a glorious early spring morning in the town of Angouleme, South-Western France. The sun shone with a renewed brightness as if to sweep away the last remnants of what had been a long, damp, miserable winter. The new warmth had brought spring flowers into bloom and given a tinge of freshness to the air. Simon Kershaw was sitting at a table outside a small cafe in one of the quiet side streets, soaking up the atmosphere and savouring his fresh morning coffee. He leaned back on the spindly metal chair and breathed out, feeling remarkably relaxed and contented.

After 20 years in the British Army he had become a civilian once again and, after a period when he had felt slightly lost, he had set up a small antique shop in Witney, Oxfordshire. Business had been difficult to start with but after some highly successful commissions from interior designers it had established itself as a sound and growing enterprise. It seemed that despite the vagaries of the economy, Brexit or pandemics, there were still plenty of people in the Cotswolds who had money and the inclination to spend it on that exquisite piece of furniture, ornament or objet d'art to complete their idyllic country properties.

He knew his good fortune was due in no small part to his beloved Vicki. They had been married for nearly 15 years and she had been his rock through good times and bad. In fact it was Vicki's connections through her old school friends that had brought the interior designers to the shop and helped establish its reputation. Simon had been despatched to France with the van to source fresh stocks of desirable items and after a successful expedition the only thing he was missing as he sat outside the cafe was the company of Vicki to share the moment. Unfortunately someone had to stay at home and run the shop.

Simon drank his coffee while the ancient yellow sandstone buildings basked in the spring sunshine. Muffled sounds of hammering and a radio came from builders working on an old house in the next street but that only seemed to emphasise the tranquillity of the atmosphere.

Suddenly the peaceful scene was interrupted: a series of shouts from the builders reached a crescendo followed immediately by an enormous crash that made the ground shake. Silence returned, accompanied by a cloud of fine, white dust creeping around the corner at the end of the street. "Bloody Hell!" thought Simon and without hesitation he was on his feet and running towards the scene. After years of military service the reaction to check for casualties was instinctive.

"Tout le monde va bien?" he shouted as he approached two dazed young men covered in dust from head to foot. "Notre ami est piege," mumbled one, nodding his head towards the hole where the front of the building had been. Simon clambered over the pile of rubble into the building where an older man he took to be the boss was trying to heave an enormous lump of masonry off a beam pinning another man by his leg. "Here we go," said Simon as he grabbed the bottom edge of the stone and together they were able to shove it to one side. With the stone out of the way, the beam could be lifted relatively easily.

As the beam moved the trapped man's face twisted with pain and he let out an agonised cry. Simon looked at the smashed leg and saw the flesh was open down to the bone. He made his handkerchief into a ball and stuffed it into the wound to stem the blood and keep out the dust. "Hold this'" he said to the boss miming the action. Then he took off his belt and with a nearby piece of wood fashioned a tourniquet to stop the man losing too much blood.

It seemed to take forever, but eventually an ambulance arrived and its crew lifted the patient onto a board carried him outside to a stretcher then roared away, sirens blaring. The injured man's sister had arrived before the ambulance so she went with him to the hospital. This left the boss with Simon whose appearance was now changed by an accumulation of dust and dirt, mingled with the odd splatter of blood.

"Merci de votre aide, Monsieur," said the man. "Oh that's quite alright," said Simon, starting to feel a little embarrassed. "Ah, I thought so, you are English, yes?" "Er yes, that's right" said Simon. The man embraced him and said "you have been very brave let me take you for a drink to thank you Monsieur." "Oh gosh!" exclaimed Simon "I rushed over here and haven't paid for my coffee in the next street. Thank you Monsieur but I must go and pay." The Frenchman would have none of it. He turned to the two young builders who by now had got over their shock and spoke quickly to one of them. The youngster nodded then sped off around the corner.

"Etienne will take care of your bill Monsieur in the meantime let me introduce myself, my name is Jean-Claude Valois. And you are?" "Simon, Simon Kershaw" he replied. By now a small crowd had gathered to stare at the debris and give their opinions to each other with much pointing and nodding. Amongst them appeared a gendarme who came over and spoke to Jean Claude. After some discussion the policeman turned to Simon and said "Thank you for your help Monsieur. Are you staying long in Angouleme?" "Actually no, I was just leaving this morning. I have to get back to Cherbourg this evening to catch the ferry." "Ah, bien, could I just trouble you to see your passport Monsieur and have a note of your address for my report."

While Simon was giving his details to the policeman Etienne had returned but was now carrying a bottle of cognac together with several glasses stuffed into various pockets. He and Jean-Claude stood a little way off while Simon spoke to the policeman then as soon as the policeman left with a friendly "Au revoir, Jean-Claude" "Au-revoir, Thierry" they closed in on Simon. "Please, just a small drink to toast our good fortune that you were here with us today," said Jean-Claude. Simon really did need to make a start on his journey but his innate good manners meant he could not refuse the gratitude of the Frenchman.

They each had a glass of cognac and Jean-Claude raised a toast to Monsieur Simon Kershaw. While they were speaking, Jean-Claude's phone rang. It was Frank's sister from the hospital: she told Jean-Claude that Frank was OK and would recover and that the stranger's first aid had stopped Frank from bleeding to death. He had saved Frank's life. This was the excuse for another round of toasts and Simon was trying to remember what the drink-drive limit was in France. After a while the situation became hopeless and the little group trooped back around the corner to the cafe where Simon received more hugs and kisses and was plied with yet more drink.

"So, you are a touriste?" Jean-Claude was saying. "No, I'm here for my work" replied Simon, raising his voice above the hubbub of conversation. "I sell antiques in England and come to France to buy more." "Ah, bien, je comprends," said Jean-Claude with a slight slurring of his words. "If you deal with old things, can you read this?" he asked, and produced a handwritten note from his pocket.

Simon took it and studied it carefully: the yellowed paper was quite brittle and clearly very old. The faded message was difficult to make out and then Simon realised it was written in Latin. "I'm sorry, Jean-Claude this is certainly very old but my Latin is not good enough to translate it. Where did it come from?" "The house we were working in today" said Jean-Claude, "we were trying to alter the cheminee – chimney, yes? And Frank knocked out that large stone. Then boom and the whole cheminee fell down. That piece of paper was inside."

"Very interesting," nodded Simon and offered the paper back to its keeper. Jean-Claude shook his head, saying "I cannot pay you for saving Frank's life and I do not have any antiquites for you to take with you. Please keep that piece of paper as a memory of what you have done here today." "Doesn't it belong to the owner of the house?" asked Simon. "Pfff" said Jean-Claude with a dismissive shrug of his shoulders "she is from Paris and would not know that paper from papier toilette." Simon laughed, carefully folded the paper and tucked it into his pocket.

Simon managed to extricate himself from the well wishers by early afternoon and walked, none too steadily, down the hill to where he'd left his van in a car park by the river. There was no way he could risk driving in his condition so instead he grabbed some food from his bag in the front of the van, raised the shutter at the back and crawled inside to fill his belly with something other than alcohol and get some sleep.

Chapter 3

It was early evening by the time he felt safe enough to drive. He hauled himself into the driving seat and set off on the six and a half-hour journey to Cherbourg. The ferry didn't sail until the following morning but he had originally planned to stop off en-route and visit friends in Le Mans. Now he would just have to drive the 600-odd kilometres straight through before parking up overnight just outside Cherbourg. He felt irritated that his schedule had been thrown off but his experiences over the years – especially in the army – had taught him to appreciate more fully the friendship and simple fellowship of others, wherever it was encountered.

After a couple of stops for food and rest, Simon arrived at the outskirts of Cherbourg at two in the morning. He found a quiet spot to park and crawled into the back of the van to grab some sleep amongst the furniture and bric-a-brac he had purchased this trip.

Next morning he awoke early and eased himself out of the van. It was still dark and he shivered slightly at the damp, chill air. He picked up his bag from the front of the van and climbed once again into the back. After a shave with his electric razor and a squirt of deodorant he put on a change of clothes. Now at least he looked more presentable even if he didn't feel like it.

The drive to the ferry was uneventful and after only a short wait this time he was safely onboard ready for the return to Portsmouth. Right he thought to himself, nothing to do for five and half hours so let's go and get breakfast. He wandered into the restaurant and ordered a full plate of eggs, bacon, sausage, beans and, tomatoes, topped off with toast and a large mug of tea. This was his first hot food since the previous morning and he attacked it with relish, ignoring the slight rolling of the ship that meant he had to eat with one hand while stopping the plate sliding off the table with the other.

With hot food inside him he began to feel distinctly improved. He strolled around the shop but saw nothing in particular to catch his eye. He bought a newspaper to pass the time but it was still full of the same trivial nonsense and claims and counter claims of politicians so it was not long before he turned to the puzzles section. That completed he looked at his watch – shit! – still another three and a half hours to go. He decided he would phone Vicki and catch up with events at home.

"Hi Sweetheart – how are things?" "Hello Darling, I'm good thanks. Did you catch up with Peter and Maria last night?" "Er, no. I got delayed in Angouleme so I didn't have time." "Oh. I thought that was why you hadn't called. What happened?" "Long story, I'll tell you when I get home this evening." "What time do you think you might be back?" "It depends what time I get clear of Portsmouth and what the traffic's like on the A34 but, with a bit of luck, I should be home around four thirty, five o clock." "Great, I'll see what I can rustle up for dinner for you." "Marvellous! See you later. Love you." "Love you too. Byee."

Even though they had been married for 15 years he still felt that same thrill whenever he spoke to Vicki. She was of medium height, slim build and had beautiful long auburn hair that he loved to run through his fingers. Her eyes were blue-grey and were her most expressive feature: they could put down anyone from thugs to senior officers with ease, yet flutter and flatter the most officious of policemen into not giving her a speeding ticket. They could also, on very rare occasions, give a glimpse of the vulnerable, uncertain little girl that lay beneath a supremely confident and efficient – almost brusque – exterior. She always looked stunning whether in heels and gown with her hair piled up on top of her head or in baggy sweatshirt and leggings cleaning old furniture: and he loved her.

The mention of Angouleme shook Simon out of his reverie and reminded him of the paper he had been given by Jean-Claude. He reached into his jacket and withdrew the note. As his knowledge of Latin hadn't progressed beyond a brief dalliance with the language whilst still in school, he turned his mind to the thing he did out of habit with the antiques that passed through his hands: he tried to work out how old it was. Angouleme prided itself on being one of the first places in Europe to manufacture paper and had a museum of paper making. From the tourist leaflets he had picked up he had learned the earliest paper-making had begun around the 12th Century, so it wasn't likely to be older than that.

The fact that it was written in Latin also gave some indication of the date. Before the 12th Century virtually everything was written in Latin. Then ordinary documents began to be written in the language of the native country until, by the 14th Century, the practice of writing in Latin had almost completely died out except for the most official or important documents. Hmm, thought Simon, I don't know what it says but I reckon its date is somewhere between 1300 and 1400, so pretty old. He also noticed the message was incomplete, as it had been partly burnt – an inevitable result of being in the chimney he concluded.

With nothing more to do, he settled back and waited for the ferry to reach port. At Portsmouth he passed through customs checks with ease and was soon headed northwards back to home and Vicki. "Hi Honey I'm home!" he yelled as he walked up the stairs into the flat over the shop. It was a clichéd thing to say but it had become at first a joke and then a habit between the couple. "Hello Darling. Come in. Can I get you a drink?" shouted Vicki from the kitchen. "Mmm whisky please! Lovely!" came the reply.

Simon dropped his travel bag on the floor and was about to slump into a chair when Vicki emerged from the kitchen, followed by an enticing aroma of cooking dinner. She came up to him walking in an almost cat-like way, put a tumbler of whisky down on the side table and then clasped her hands around the back of his neck. "So, has my brave soldier come back with lots of goodies to sell to make me a fabulously wealthy woman?" she asked. "There's a couple of painted armoires, a really nice mirror and some interesting figures," he answered "but nothing that's going to make us millionaires." She giggled and they kissed. "You'll just have to find some other way to make it up to me," she laughed and then disappeared back into the kitchen.

"How long before dinner Honey?" he asked. "About half an hour" "OK I'm going for a shower." With that Simon took a long gulp of Scotch and headed for the bathroom. The shower was hot and soothing and for a while he just stood and let it run down his body. When he had finished he put all his travel clothes into the laundry basket, dressed in pyjama bottoms and T shirt, pulled on a towelling dressing gown and went back into the lounge.

Within a moment Vicki appeared from the kitchen with a dinner of roast pork, roast potatoes, vegetables and apple sauce. This was followed by home-made raspberry pavlova, coffee cheese and biscuits.

After dinner they settled down together in the large, old, sofa: Vicki resting her legs on his and Simon gently massaging her stockinged feet. The shop had been pretty quiet while he'd been away, Vicki said although she had sold a pair of brass candlesticks and the large, wingback chair that had been hanging around for months. "So tell me why you didn't make it to Peter and Maria's" she asked. "What happened in Angouleme?" Simon explained about the collapsed building and the injured man and how he'd had to stay around afterwards to deal with questions from the police and so on. He didn't mention the drinking session as being the reason he couldn't leave earlier as he knew Vicki would simply have, ever so charmingly, declined the hospitality and driven away.

"There was one thing though," said Simon and he went over to the coat stand and drew the ancient paper from his jacket. "It was hidden in the chimney of the house that collapsed. Jean-Claude gave it to me as a sort of memento." Vicki looked it over as Simon explained how he'd worked out how old it might be. "What's it say?" she asked. "I don't know, I can't read Latin." "Why don't you ask Tim about it" she suggested. "If you can find out what it says, it might be worth something," she added. "That's a good idea," replied Simon. "I'll go and see him after I've unloaded the van tomorrow."

Next day Simon – with some help from Vicki – unloaded his latest purchases from the van. They made some rearrangements to the stock layout in the shop and changed a few prices around then Simon set off for Oxford.

Chapter 4

Oxford was only a short drive from Witney but the difficulties and cost of parking in the ancient city meant Simon and Vicki tended to keep their visits to a minimum. Simon had already planned to do a few errands there so going to see his friend Tim was no extra effort. With his jobs completed, he strolled into the antiquarian bookshop where Tim worked at a little after midday. "Hello Tim. How are you?" he asked the young man behind the cash register.

"Simon! It's good to see you! How are you, you old fart?" Tim Woodruff was in his early twenties – about half Simon's age. They had met through Witney Rugby Club where Simon had turned out for the Veterans and Tim for the Club's 4th XV. Simon's realisation that he was now a 'veteran' player had been something of a disappointment to him – but a huge source of amusement to Tim, who still enjoyed teasing Simon whenever the opportunity presented itself.

Despite their age difference they had many things in common: a shared love of rugby and beer was obvious, but Tim was an archaeology graduate and both he and Simon were keen students of history. Tim's interest was perhaps understandable but Simon's wider interest in history had developed as an extension of his interest in military history.

That in turn had been inspired by an incident during his service in Afghanistan. An Afghan said his grandfather was upset because British troops has caused much destruction in his village and Simon, under orders to win hearts and minds amongst the locals, duly paid a visit to the old man to smooth things over. It turned out the destruction in question had happened in the late 1870s during the Second Afghan War. Memories were long in that part of the world and it drove home to Simon the importance of understanding history in dealing with conflicts.

Since then an interest in history had helped enormously in running the antique shop. His knowledge enabled shrewd judgements in the purchase of stock and gave him the ability to offer sound advice to customers seeking to furnish or decorate their own homes.

Tim had been working in the antiquarian bookshop since graduation. He still sought a position as an archaeologist but the opportunities were few and far between and competition for them was fierce. At least here he was able to earn a living and combine it with an opportunity to study a variety of ancient and modern texts on historical subjects.

"Look here you cheeky oik," said Simon. "I've got a very old piece of paper here with some writing on it in Latin. It could be some medieval love letter or something and may be worth a few quid so if you could kindly translate it, I might be able to supply you with some beer." "Ooo! That sounds important – why didn't you say something?" joked Tim. "Let me take a copy of it and I'll have a look at it later. I can bring it over at the weekend if you like?"

"Thanks that'd be great" nodded Simon. "You don't have to come out to Witney, you can just email it to me if you like," he added and then, as an afterthought: "Where are you staying at the moment?" This last question related to Tim's living accommodation: a caravan he towed around the county behind an old Land Rover called Florence. "As it happens, I'm near Witney at the moment" said Tim, "so I could call in on Saturday and we could go for that beer you promised." "Hmm, I suppose you'd like to come round for a bite to eat first?" asked Simon. "Well that would be very kind of you, thanks." Simon laughed, Tim's cooking was, at best, rudimentary and the opportunity to enjoy one of Vicki's dinners was one he took whenever he could. "OK, see you Saturday, around six?" "Looking forward to it" answered Tim.

That evening after dinner, Tim pulled out the photocopy of Simon's paper and started to translate it. As he worked his casual curiosity grew. The paper read "....safe in France...three ships must take everything as soon as possible. The ships will go to ...." then more missing text then "of all, can be hidden and kept secret by our loyal friend over the water who holds the nails of the Cross..." It certainly wasn't a love letter or some idle chatter amongst friends. It sounded more like specific instructions of some importance. There was nothing more to be done he thought. Perhaps Simon could shed some more light on the subject at the weekend and with that he packed his papers away and turned on the TV.

Saturday came and after Tim had finished his stint at the Bookshop he drove back towards Witney in Florence. The weather had been pretty good after what seemed like weeks of rain and his thoughts turned idly towards the longer days and warmer weather to come. Then he began thinking about what delights Vicki might have prepared for dinner. He always enjoyed his time with Simon and Vicki, not just because of the great food and conversation but also, though he found it hard to admit it, because he had a little bit of a crush on Vicki even though she was easily old enough to be his mother.

He stopped at the off licence to buy a bottle of wine and then found a place to park Florence not too far from the antiques shop. For the next two weeks his caravan was sited on a farm just a couple of miles outside Witney so if he was unable to drive home he could easily get a taxi or, if the weather was OK he could walk. Simon came down to let him into the flat and he greeted Vicki with a cheery "Hi" as he reached the top of the stairs.

As he had anticipated, the meal – home-made beef Wellington followed by his favourite key lime pie – was excellent, the drinks generous and the company truly enjoyable. As they sat around after dinner Simon said "where's my Latin translation?" "Oh yes – I nearly forgot" said Tim and walked over to the Edwardian coat stand at the top of the stairs to get the translation from his jacket. He passed it to Simon saying "It's not the medieval love letter you were perhaps expecting but it is quite curious."

Simon read the translation. "I see what you mean" he said. "It reads more like a set of shipping instructions" he added as he passed it to Vicki. She studied the translation and said "It's not ordinary shipping instructions though, is it? I mean why would you say it can be hidden and kept secret by our friend etc etc?" that sounds more like smuggling to me." They agreed she had a point.

"You think it's smuggling something like wine or tobacco?" questioned Tim. Simon had taken the paper back and was looking at it with increased interest. "It could be" he mused "but it doesn't sound like part of a regular trade – more like a one-off. See here where it says must take everything as soon as possible, that's a going out of business thing to say." They wondered what could be so important that all of it had to be taken at once and then kept hidden. Vicki had retrieved the original paper and after looking at it and Tim's translation said "see here where it says something about safe in France? There's a bit missing, so might it actually have read not safe in France? Is that why they had to move whatever it was?"

Tim looked at the original again and agreed "yes, you could be right. It could have said not safe in France." It was indeed a strange note they agreed. It was written in Latin, denoting the hand of someone relatively well educated, so no ordinary thief or smuggler. It suggested the operation was one-time only and was caused by some event happening across France.

"How old do you think the note is?" asked Vicki. Simon began explaining about the introduction of paper-making narrowing the date at the earliest to the 12th Century when Tim exclaimed "Bloody Hell – I think I know!" Simon and Vicki turned towards him and now he felt a little embarrassed by his outburst and tried to pass off his idea as a sort of joke "I thought it could be the Knights Templar shifting their treasure out of France. I mean the dates fit, it's a one-off and the note's written in Latin" he reasoned. Simon gave him a distinctly cynical look but Vicki sat upright greeting the suggestion with enthusiasm.

Simon looked at Tim and said "nice idea old son, but this note came from Angouleme which is even further away from Paris than La Rochelle where the Templars had their own fleet of ships." "Explain to me about the Knights Templar" demanded Vicki, so Simon and Tim explained how King Philip of France issued an order in October 1307 for the arrest of the Templar order of Knights and the seizure of their considerable wealth, most of which was believed to be in Paris. But one of the great mysteries was that the Templar's treasure had never been found.

"If you were trying to escape with your treasure, would you take it to La Rochelle where the King might be expecting you, or would you go somewhere else?" asked Vicki. Simon had to concede that in the circumstances it would probably have been a good idea to avoid La Rochelle. "There we are then" Vicki grinned triumphantly. "All you two have to do now is find out where they took it!" "Ha ha – we know where they took it Mrs Kershaw" said Simon, grinning at Vicki's smugness. "They took it to their chum who" and he glanced again at the translation " their chum over the water who holds the nails of the cross!"

The dining and conversation had lasted longer than expected so before long Tim took his leave, deciding to walk the couple of miles in the moonlight back to his caravan. He would come back tomorrow to fetch Florence.

The mysterious paper was largely forgotten by everyone until later the next week when Tim was having a coffee break with his boss, the bookshop's owner John Impey. It was one of those things that just comes up in casual conversation. Tim mentioned the note and how they, half-jokingly, thought it might relate to the lost treasure of the Templars. "The trick would be to work out who the person is who holds the nails of the cross" said Tim. John had been considering the description and said "well, as you know, religious relics of any kind were big business in the 11th and 12th Centuries. Churches and religious institutions that had relics attracted paying pilgrims and the bigger and better the relic the more money they could make."

"Were people really that gullible?" mused Tim. "Oh it was taken very seriously. Very seriously indeed" said John. "Where it says over the water, where do you think that might have been?" continued Tim. "Hmm, assuming it was October I wouldn't have fancied sailing anywhere too far at that time of year in the kind of boats they had" said John. Back in the late seventies before he had become a respectable book dealer John's life had a certain la dolce vita style. He had crewed a yacht that made several return journeys from the Dorset coast down through the Bay of Biscay to the Iberian Peninsula and on to Morocco. He decided to curtail his voyages following one particularly rough storm in Biscay and a tricky encounter with a French customs vessel. But he knew about sailing the French coast at that time of year.

"My guess is they would have wanted to clear the Continent completely to avoid Philip's spies" said John. "Sailing south wouldn't have been very pleasant so that leaves heading north and a lucky sprint across the Channel." "Ah Hah!" said Tim. The thought that if there was treasure it was entirely possible for it to have been hidden in Britain was an appealing one.

On his way home after work he phoned Simon to tell him about his conversation with John. It was Vicki that answered. "Is he there?" "He's out the back doing something to the van," said Vicki "can I give him a message?" Tim explained the conversation with John and the strong possibility that any treasure might in fact be in the UK. "Thanks I'll tell him when he comes in" said Vicki.

She relayed Tim's message and Simon thought about it for a while. "If he's right, we need to find somewhere that holds the nails of the Cross" he said. They looked through reference books and searched the net for anywhere in the UK claiming to have nails of the Cross but found nothing. Then Vicki had an idea: "when that note said holds the nails of the Cross could that also be translated as bears the nails of the cross?" "What do you mean?" asked Simon "It's just a thought" she continued "but what if it didn't mean literally holding the nails but displaying a representation of them in something like a flag or a coat of arms?"

The idea was a good one but after another fruitless internet search it was Simon's turn to have a good idea. He sent off an email to the College of Arms in London, asking for details of any coats of arms dating from the 11th or 12th Centuries that might incorporate the nails of the Cross into their designs.

The weeks passed and then one day as Simon was checking his emails in the shop he found a reply from the College of Arms. A Miss Julie Lyons sent a long missive about the origins of arms, how they used various devices etc. etc. Right at the end of her communication she finished with two sentences that were perhaps just what Simon wanted to hear: "Of course the nails could well appear – in heraldic language – as piles, or long thin wedge shapes emerging from the top of the shield and converging to a point near the base. The coat of arms that springs to mind with three piles, perhaps representing the three nails of the cross, is that of the de Bryan family who were located in the West Country. I hope this is of interest, yours sincerely etc."

When Vicki came in later on he said "Hello Darling, do you fancy a bit of an adventure?" "What do you mean?" He read out the vital part of the email from the College of Arms. "And that's not all," he added "I've been looking at the West Country and there are two places called Hazelbury Bryan and Torbryan which seem definitely worth investigating. They were both settlements belonging to the de Bryan family – and in 1307 they would have been within easy sailing distance from Angouleme. We could take the van and look for some more stock at the same time?"

"Hmm," said Vicki. "We haven't had any time off together for ages, let's leave the van and instead find a nice hotel for a couple of days."

Chapter 5

"Stop worrying! Everything will be fine!" Simon and Vicki had put their luggage in the car and were just doing their final checks before heading to the West Country. Normally Vicki's mother and father were able to come over from Cheltenham to mind the shop but as they were away visiting friends in Canada Vicki had persuaded Simon to ask Tim if he could help out. Tim was doing his best to be reassuring: "look everything has got a price ticket on it, I know I can only offer five percent maximum discount and if there's any questions I can phone you. Now go away and have a good time!"

It was fortunate Tim had been able to get the time off from his own job in Oxford. He had been chatting with his boss John Impey explaining Simon and Vicki's 'quest' and John had been really helpful. "You and Claire are familiar with running this place," he said "which makes it easy for any one of us to take time off. But it's more difficult when the place is run by a couple." Tim was going to take unpaid leave and any compensation for his loss of earnings was a matter for agreement – probably in cash – between him and Simon.

Eventually Simon and Vicki set off in the BMW towards Oxford and the A34. At Oxford they turned south onto the A34 and headed towards Newbury. Both felt that almost illicit thrill of taking time off from their work and the conversation was light and happy. Gradually they fell into a relaxed silence and Vicki gazed idly at the rolling Berkshire countryside passing by while Simon negotiated his way past the lorries and slower moving cars on the road. In what seemed like no time at all they had passed over the M4 motorway and by-passed Newbury. At the junction with the A303, one of the main routes to the West Country, they turned off towards Andover and all points west.

They had passed Stonehenge many times but today, as they were officially on holiday, they decided to stop and have a look around the iconic monument. They bought their tickets and meandered, hand-in-hand, around the ancient stones. "Simon," began Vicki "what do you actually hope to find when we get to Hazelbury Bryan?" Simon stared off into the distance and considered the question: "I don't know really. I suppose when you've been in a country in conflict you see the efforts people will go to in order to protect the things they value most. If this note is real – and if we've understood it correctly – it would be quite something to find the treasure the Knights risked their lives to protect. In a funny way it would be keeping the faith with fellow soldiers." Vicki said nothing but just entwined her arm a little tighter with his and leaned her head into his shoulder. He's still hurting, she thought.

They checked in to their farmhouse bed and breakfast near Hazelbury Bryan later that day and went for a walk, stopping at the Antelope pub on the edge of the village. Simon got out the notes he had put together before their journey: "Hmm, it says here that the manor wasn't bought by Sir Guy de Bryan until 1361. I didn't realize, but that's over 50 years after the knights would have left France with their treasure," he mused. "Still, we'll have a look at the Church tomorrow and see if that tells us anything." The following day they parked in the little car park opposite Hazelbury Bryan school and wandered into the local Church.

A brief inspection of the pretty little parish church failed to show any clues that might help their quest. "This says the church dates mostly from the 15th Century," said Simon. "What with that and the manor only being bought half a century later than the treasure would have been moved, I'm beginning to think this isn't the right place." Vicki gave him a look of sympathetic disappointment but Simon, ever the optimist, said "no problem! If it was easy someone else would have found this stuff. Besides, we haven't explored Torbryan yet and I've a feeling that is closer to the right dates for us."

They spent the rest of the day doing a little sightseeing and just taking the opportunity to relax and catch up on their reading. The next day after a hearty breakfast they left their farmhouse accommodation and headed further south towards Torbryan. After a rather leisurely journey through picturesque Devon villages, they found a hotel on the coast not too far from Torbryan. Dawn the next day was a rather wet affair, with drizzle and squally showers blowing in off the Atlantic. Peering through the rain as it was dispersed so silently and efficiently by the BMW's windscreen wipers, they drove down narrow high-sided lanes towards Torbryan and the local Holy Trinity Church. Just opposite the church was the Old Church House Inn. "Brilliant!" observed Simon "Let's go in for a pint and dry out by the fire." It transpired that Holy Trinity Church was built in the 15th Century, again much too late for it to have received any visitors in 1307 but the pub itself was a different matter.

"Apparently this pub dates back to the 13th Century," said Simon – "which is perfect from a date point of view. It's also supposed to be.... haunted! Wooooo!" he laughed, waving his arms around like a cartoon ghost. "Oh Simon, behave" scolded a slightly disapproving Vicki. "Do you think it has any connection with Guy de Bryan and the treasure?" "Treasure?" came the voice of another customer, alerted by Simon's ghost impressions. "Er, yes, we wondered if anyone has ever found any treasure here," replied Vicki. "No, shouldn't think so" said the stranger. "This place does have a lot of ghosts" – he looked at Simon – "but it's been explored from top to bottom by all types of folk over the years and, far as I know, no-one has ever found any great treasure – or if they did, it was so long ago it's well gone by now," he laughed.

They chatted for some time about the pub and the various manifestations reported within its walls and then, without revealing anything about the fragment of paper or their search for Templar relics, they once again mentioned the name of Sir Guy de Bryan. "Well of course the de Bryan family are all over Devon," explained their new friend. "Oh, I don't know if it's any help to you, but they've got their coat of arms on a church window near here." "That would be interesting," agreed Simon. "Can you tell us where it is please?" added Vicki. "Slapton Church, it's about 20 miles from here, down on the coast the other side of Dartmouth."

The couple made their way to Slapton, arriving in the village in the early afternoon. They parked in the car park of the Queens Arms pub and walked into the church. After a little searching they found the stained glass windows showing the shields of arms of Guy, Lord Bryan and those of his two sons Guy and William. They gazed at the shields, with the three nails – or piles – coming to a point. "It's odd isn't it?" said Vicki "that the nails are blue and the background is gold, when I would have thought the nails would have been gold against a blue sky?"

"Yes," agreed Simon somewhat absently. "It says here the altar was dedicated in 1318 – which would fit if you had spent around ten or eleven years making a hiding place for treasure and then building a church on top of it." "Do you really think this is where the knights could have brought their treasure to hide it from Philip?" queried Vicki. "Well it's certainly possible," said Simon "but I don't know how we would set about trying to prove it." They sat and reflected on the possibility. Eventually Simon stirred and said "We're fairly close to the beach here, so I think it would have been a simple matter to have brought anything straight up from the shore and placed it in here. Let's go and see the beach."

They drove the short distance to the beach and parked in a car park right on the shore. A large stone monument was sited next to the car park and they wandered over to examine the inscriptions on its sides. It was a memorial to the hundreds of American soldiers and sailors who died during Exercise Tiger, a training operation staged in April 1944 in preparation for the D Day landings in Normandy in June 1944. On April 27th craft carrying troops towards the beach were accidently fired upon by American land-based forces due to a mix-up in timings. This resulted in hundreds of men being killed or wounded. In the early hours of the following day, landing craft waiting offshore were attacked by a passing group of German fast-attack E boats with two craft being sunk and two others seriously damaged. Over the course of those two days, a total of 749 men were killed.

The light rain and drizzle of earlier in the day had returned, adding to the gloom surrounding this sombre memorial. Vicki was feeling the cold damp of this early spring weather and she could see Simon was visibly moved by the story of so many lives lost in the effort to free Europe from Nazi tyranny. "Simon, I'd like to go home, take me back to Witney please." They climbed back into the BMW and drove back in silence for some considerable way before Simon's mood lifted.

Chapter 6

Back in Witney, Simon and Vicki both felt an air of disappointment. The whole adventure had started quite casually but the clues they had gleaned had fuelled a rising excitement and sense of expectation. Now it felt like they had only been fooling themselves. "I checked and the Guy de Bryan whose shield was on the window in Slapton Church wasn't born until 1320," said Simon flatly. "I've also been thinking about that beach as well," he continued. "I just don't think you would land ships in such an exposed spot and then wait around in broad daylight until finding somewhere to unload a precious cargo without people finding out about it."

As the days passed, the quest for the Templar treasure became largely forgotten, pushed to the back of their minds by more pressing needs such as the need to sell stock and earn money. The shop seemed to have a charmed existence as whenever funds were falling low something happened to refill the coffers. Today was no exception, as into the shop walked a young married couple to be met by a squeal of delight from Vicki: "Sarah! Oh my Darling! How are you?" the two women embraced while Simon and the other man stood, looking at each other in embarrassment.

"Oh Simon this is Sarah! You remember – she came to our wedding." Simon didn't remember, as he'd met so many people that day who were friends of Vicki whom he'd never heard of or seen before – or since. "Hello Sarah, how do you do" he said politely, giving her a strong handshake and a warm smile . Sarah introduced her husband Martin. They had married three years ago and were now busy putting the finishing touches to the large house they had bought near Monmouth, just over the border in Wales.

"We heard Simon had left the army and you were running an antique shop so we thought we'd come and say hello," explained Sarah. Martin was a commodities trader and after a particularly good year had bought a run-down Georgian mansion in the middle of nowhere not long after they were married. "The builders have finally finished so now we've got to find some furniture to put in it" said Martin.

The girls chatted about old times and what had happened to others from their time at Cheltenham Ladies College and eventually they got around to the business of the day – buying furniture. It soon became clear that while Martin had the funds it was Sarah who had the eye for good quality antiques. First she chose the huge mahogany dining table – plus chairs – that had for perhaps too long been the centre piece in the shop. That was followed by a large Welsh dresser in pine "perfect for the kitchen" a linen press and, from the yard at the rear of the shop, four cast iron posts for conversion into lamp posts along the drive.

Sarah and Vicki began negotiating hard over the final price until it looked like they might descend into an argument. Simon, who had been keeping out of the discussion, defused the situation by offering to deliver the items to their home near Monmouth free of charge. Sarah knew a good deal when she saw it and agreed, allowing everyone to be friends once again. "I can offset the cost by searching for some new stock while I'm over there" Simon explained to Vicki later on. "Besides, we've got some holes to fill in the shop now" he added.

He arranged the delivery for the day before an antique auction happening in Abergavenny. This would give him plenty of opportunity to deliver Sarah's furniture and then make the half-hour or so journey to Abergavenny and view the items before the auction. Simon would sleep overnight in the back of the van – as he had done many times previously. He could stay in a bed and breakfast or a hotel for the night but sometimes he actually quite enjoyed his own company sleeping in the van. In a way it felt like he was keeping in touch with his time in the military.

The day arrived and Simon and Vicki were up early to load Sarah's purchases into the van. Simon came back into the flat for breakfast and to pick up his bag and then he was off to Monmouthshire. It was a glorious sunny morning and he was enjoying the drive. The long, seemingly endless, walls of Cotswold stone bounding the fields on the first part of the journey gave way to the industrialised outskirts of Gloucester which in turn transformed into the hilly woodlands of the Forest of Dean.

Although the trees were not yet in leaf after their winter slumbers, the signs of spring were growing stronger everywhere. Daffodils punctuated roadsides and gardens along the way and catkins were dangling from hazel bushes everywhere. Simon loved being outdoors and he had been surprised at how much the antiques shop had provided the opportunity to indulge this passion. In effect he was earning money driving around the countryside.

He followed the winding road down into Monmouth and then, after carefully following the Sat Nav directions, found his way onto the single track road that led to Sarah and Martin's mansion. Sarah was there on her own – Martin was in London for a meeting – but they soon managed to offload the furniture and get it into place to Sarah's satisfaction. They had performed an amazing restoration job and the house was indeed magnificent but it was too remote and still, in Simon's view, too empty, to be a home. In this secluded location a house this large needed cooks, gardeners, kitchen staff and above all children, he thought.

His delivery completed, Simon set off for the auction rooms in Abergavenny. The Sat Nav seemed to take him on every high-banked, single track road in the area so it wasn't until he reached a filling station on one of the wider roads that he could buy some sandwiches for a lunch on the move.

In Abergavenny he found one or two items he thought would be worth a bid but the good quality items were a little thin on the ground. There had been a time when Wales had been a rich hunting ground for antiques, especially sturdy, vernacular pieces. These had come from farmhouses whose contents had been sold on the death of the farmer or his wife – their descendants having moved away to more modern houses and easier, better-paid occupations. Ironically the farms had been amalgamated into larger units and the now redundant traditional farmhouses and outbuildings were sold to those who had made their fortunes in more urban surroundings.

He was tempted just to head home and make his bids by telephone tomorrow but he realised if he was successful it would mean another journey to collect the items. Instead he left the auction rooms to check out the antique shops in town and then buy a Chinese take away to enjoy in the back of the van. With hot evening meal in hand, he returned to the van, drove a short way out of town and found a quiet lay-by to settle down for the night.

Next morning he was back at the auction rooms and ready for business. Auctions can be strange animals where sometimes the bidding is intense and sometimes the auctioneer struggles to get any interest at all. Today Simon was in luck: he recognised two of the people he had seen in antique shops in town yesterday but it seemed there was little enthusiasm for bidding. The chest of drawers he had his eye on was his for next to nothing, as was the marble-topped Victorian washstand and the Edwardian sideboard, although slightly more expensive, was also his for a very reasonable figure.

He settled up with the auctioneer, got one of their staff to help him load up, and set off back towards Monmouth and home. Feeling quite pleased with his day, he was driving back up the steep switchback road from Monmouth into the Forest of Dean when coming the other way he saw a white Transit van – and on the side of it was Sir Guy de Bryan's coat of arms! Caught completely by surprise he managed a sort of half-hearted wave at the driver and then beeped the horn as the vehicle sped downhill in the opposite direction. There was nowhere to stop and turn around and besides, he reasoned, by the time I've turned around he'll be long gone.

It almost seemed this as if this was a deliberate act to stop him enjoying his successes at the auction. Simon drove the rest of the way home in a contemplative mood. "Hi Honey I'm home," he shouted up the stairs on his return to Witney. He would unload tomorrow: this evening he was looking forward to a shower and dinner with Vicki.

As they ate, Simon gave Vicki his impressions of Sarah's house and told her of his successes at the auction. He didn't mention seeing the coat of arms until they were relaxing after dinner. "He went past so fast, I just didn't have time to do anything about it. If I could only have got the phone number I could have asked him more about it," he added. "There was a number on the side of the van?" queried Vicki. "Yes, next to the crest but it was too quick for me to see it."

"Ah hah! I have the solution to your problem" said Vicki triumphantly "give me the keys to the van." Simon looked at her quizzically and handed over the keys. Within a few moments she had returned from the van, shivering slightly after being out in the cold night air. "You've forgotten about this" she announced proudly and opened her hand to reveal a small computer card. "Of course! The bloody dash camera!" said Simon. Vicki laughed "you poor old dinosaur, fancy forgetting that" and they loaded the card into the computer. Scrolling through the recordings from the journey they eventually got to the white van appearing around the corner, sporting the de Bryan coat of arms.

Unfortunately, a combination of dirt on the van and the angle of the recording made it difficult to read the signwriting it carried but there was enough to make out the telephone area code. "That's great – at least we can find out where it came from" said Simon. "You are wonderful" he said to Vicki and kissed her. "I know" she said "come to bed.

Chapter 7

Simon looked up the telephone dialling code they had taken from the dash camera image of the white van. 01994 was a place called St Clears which, it turned out, was in West Wales. A few days later he was chatting to Tim on the phone and mentioned seeing the van and tracing it to St Clears. "What? You're kidding!" exclaimed Tim. "Why? What do you mean?" asked Simon. Tim had been researching the Templar treasure story and the whole mythology that had grown up around the subject. Theories ranged from the plausible to the outlandish, but a location that featured strongly centred around Rosslyn Chapel in Midlothian, Scotland.

"So what? I don't see the connection?" said Simon. "It may just be a coincidence, but the family name of the owners of Rosslyn Chapel is Sin..clair" announced Tim. "Don't you see? St Clears and Sinclair are variations of the same name." Simon agreed it sounded interesting and Tim, enthused by this latest occurrence, promised to find out more about St Clears.

It didn't take long for him to get in touch with Simon once again: "You'll never believe this but St Clears is named after the castle in the village – the castle of the Norman Knight Henry St Clair, Baron of Rosslyn. Not only that but St Clears castle was built in the mid 1100s so would have existed when the Knights Templar left France in 1307 whereas Rosslyn chapel didn't exist until a 100 years after that date. It would have been a long time to keep priceless treasures hidden in temporary accommodation. I think the place is definitely worth a look."

"I take your point," said Simon "but what about the shield of the de Bryan family? Have you found any connection to that?" "Er, well not yet" admitted Tim "but I'm sure if we go down there we could ask around. After all, that's where your mysterious white van came from" he reasoned.

Simon told Vicki about Tim's 'find' and she laughed. "I don't know which of you is worse" she said, then added "so when are you going to go down there?" "Don't you want to come?" he asked. "We can't both go – especially before Mum and Dad get back from Canada – why don't you take Tim? A boys day out would be good for both of you." Simon duly arranged with Tim that they would take a day off mid-week to make the journey to St Clears. It looked like a three-hour run so to make it worthwhile they would leave early and, most probably, return late.

So it was they were leaving Witney at six thirty in the morning on the following Wednesday. They chose to go via Gloucester and along the A40 route to Carmarthen and St Clears rather than the simpler way along the M4 motorway. Although the motorway was probably faster it was likely, they agreed, to be far less interesting than passing through the countryside of the Welsh Marches and South and West Wales.

The area close to the Welsh border was not unknown to Simon, not just because of his delivery to Monmouth, but also because he had spent some time in a place called Sennybridge, near Brecon. This unassuming little village was home to a large military camp. It was situated in the heart of the mountainous Brecon Beacons National Park and was a location of choice for sending soldiers on arduous cross-country survival training exercises.

On a sunny day the open mountain landscape was a lovely place to be. It looked a little like the Scottish Highlands and the only sound would be the odd sheep or the varying song of a skylark carried on the breeze. But that could all change so very quickly and the unprepared could find themselves in trouble on a cold, exposed hillside with no shelter and precious little visibility. It was a place, Simon thought, that could sort the men from the boys.

As they passed through Brecon, Sennybridge, Llandovery and a handful of other places the topics of discussion included rugby and the merits of the present Welsh and English teams as well as the architecture of the buildings they passed and even the obligatory sheep jokes. The one thing Tim didn't mention was Simon's military career. He knew Simon had risen to the rank of Major during his time and had been well liked and respected by colleagues and the troops that served under him. But his experiences on active service in Iraq and Afghanistan had had a profound effect on him. He had resigned his commission and in civilian life he talked about his experiences as little as possible.

They arrived in the county town of Carmarthen and a short while later were taking the exit off a bypass into the village of St Clears. Arriving at a T junction, the choice was whether to turn left into the village, or right towards the old castle. It was coming up to ten o' clock and Simon turned to Tim and said "it's a bit early for coffee. Shall we go and look at this castle first?"

Chapter 8

The open water between Normandy and Cornwall was no place for the flat-bottomed coq ships of Philippe de Chretien's convoy especially during October, when storms could easily swamp such heavily laden open boats. Mercifully, and by the grace of God, they were spared any such storms and at night a full moon helped to light their way. After a day and a half they rounded the tip of Cornwall and set a north-easterly course seeking a castle on the Welsh shore set on a headland between the rivers Taf and Corran.

They sailed on, passing the island of Lundy to their right and seeing the island of Caldy appearing to their left. Ahead lay a long sweep of golden yellow sandy beach with dunes behind. "Not far now," said Phillipe to Bernard. "We look for the estuary that marks the end of those sands." Sure enough, at the end of the line of sand dunes there lay a river estuary and just visible in the distance a castle, almost gleaming white in the low autumn sunshine.

Bernard was relieved they were now back within the shelter of land but this was mixed with some trepidation at the reception they might meet. As they approached the castle, he could see there was a harbour that allowed ships to tie up right at the foot of the castle walls. Most ships moored in the river Corran to unload onto the open ground adjoining what appeared to be a monastery but, by manoeuvring around into the river Taf, there was a dock directly under the castle walls. Above this dock there was a stout timber beam projecting from the castle wall which served as a crane, allowing cargo to be raised straight into the castle itself.

The three ships drew alongside each other and dropped anchor just a little way off the dockside. "First we must try to do as little as possible to draw the attention of the townsfolk to us," Phillipe instructed. "Keep all your weapons on the ships. Make sure you can reach them if necessary but keep them hidden under cover. Just take a dagger with you but keep it hidden under your shirt."

A small boat was lowered and six of the knights made their way towards the castle – and sanctuary for their precious cargo.

In the castle itself, 27 year old Guy de Bryan was concerned about the health of his father the Lord de Bryan of Laugharne. At 56 years old his father was no longer in the first flush of youth yet neither was he truly old. The concern of Guy was that within a single night, his father's left hand seemed to have withered and his speech had become slurred and unintelligible. Guy sent word to the monks from Aedes Christi, the monastery across the river Corran from the castle, to attend his father.

At the instruction of the Father Abbot – a personal friend of Lord de Bryan – brother Jerome had come up to the castle and examined the ailing Lord. "He hath suffered an apoplexy," diagnosed the monk. He knew there was little he could do to help the stricken man but, on seeing the anxiety in the patient's son, he prescribed an established homeopathic remedy – powdered bone from the skull of a deceased person. "I will attend my duties in the monastery and return later today with the prepared medicine" he said to Guy.

Guy was deeply troubled. His father had been a fearless soldier – he had been on a Crusade to the Holy land with Prince, now King, Edward when he was 21 and just five years later had retaken Laugharne castle from the forces of Llewelyn ap Gruffudd during a rebellion of the Welsh princes. But he was also a deeply religious man and an expert in administering fairness and justice to the indigenous people of his Lordship. As a result, Laugharne had been little troubled by the last Welsh rebellion when Guy was just three years old.

Immigrants had arrived and settled in Laugharne from King Edward's domains on the other side of the Channel, so the market of the prosperous little town rang with voices not just in the native Welsh language but also its close Celtic relatives of Breton, Norman-French and Flemish. And while many local people discretely followed their own Celtic pagan beliefs, Christianity had been the chief religion since Roman times so the arrival of the monks in Laugharne, encouraged by Guy's father, had further acted as a unifying force between native Welsh and their Norman rulers.

As his father now sat in his chamber, physically weakened and unable to speak, Guy felt the weight of responsibility as Lord of Laugharne beginning to descend upon his shoulders. Whilst he was pondering how best he should exercise his impending duties, a servant arrived. "Three ships have moored below the castle and they have requested to speak with the Lord" he announced, somewhat nervously. "Tell them he cannot see them. Ask them what it is they want and we shall deal with it in due course," ordered Guy.

The servant withdrew but within a short while reappeared. Guy was normally of good humour but his father's health preoccupied his thoughts so he was terse in his response "what is it now?" he snapped. "Forgive me sir but their leader says he was with your father in the Holy Land and has urgent business with him of the utmost importance." Guy had thought the ships were just more merchants from Flanders seeking to trade or perhaps settle in the area but this was different. He was intrigued to meet someone who might have fought alongside his father in the Crusades so he softened a little. "Tell them his Lordship is indisposed," ordered Guy "and that I will receive them in the Great Hall."

"Bonjour, j m'appelle Guy de Bryan. Et vous?" "Bonjour, j m'appelle Philippe de Chretien. We are knights of the Order of Knights Templar and we humbly and urgently request the assistance of Guy de Bryan, Lord of Laugharne." Philippe explained the hurried departure from France and the arrests by King Philip of those who had remained behind. Both men studied the other's reactions closely, trying to decide each if the other could be trusted. Guy took it upon himself to offer the assistance of his father "how can Laugharne help the Templar Knights?"

Philippe looked around to check that no-one else could be privy to their conversation, then he came close to Guy and, almost in a whisper, said "We carry the wealth of our Order which must be preserved for us to continue our work, but also..." and he paused, looking into the young man's eyes for any signs of treachery or disloyalty in his soul. "But also, we carry relics from the Temple of Solomon that must be hidden and protected until the end of days."

Guy was taken aback "But why do you come here? Why not to the King? Or to some other, greater, place than Laugharne?" "There are many good reasons why we are here," replied Philippe. "Secrecy is our most important quest and few of our pursuers will think to seek us in the land of the Cymrics. Trust not to betray our secret is also essential, and the Lord Bryan is a Crusader whose very coat of arms portrays the three nails of the cross. He is a true friend of the brotherhood and can be trusted. And finally," he added "there is safety. Laugharne is difficult to reach from France without being seen. It lies within a day's ride of Knights in the commandery at Templeton and has many loyal to the brotherhood at St Clairs less than two leagues to the north."

Guy considered this astonishing request. "It is, as you say, my father that is known to you. He has been recently stricken with apoplexy and is much enfeebled, but he is still Lord. I will take him to you that you may seek his blessing." The two men made their way to Lord de Bryan's chamber. "My Lord," began Guy to his father "this is Philippe de Chretien, he is a Templar Knight who seeks your assistance in a vital task." "Guy, my old friend, it saddens me to see you like this" Philippe interjected. The Lord of Laugharne stared at the man before him and reached out his arms to embrace him.

The younger de Bryan looked puzzled: "we first met when your father was on his way to the Crusades" explained Philippe. "But it is perhaps 20 years since last we were in each other's company."

Chapter 9

At the T junction in St Clears Simon and Tim turned right, heading towards the castle of the Norman Knight. If either of them thought it slightly ridiculous to travel all this way for the flimsiest of reasons neither of them said so. They drove along a street made narrower by rows of parked cars and almost missed the opening amongst the terrace of houses that led to what had once been the castle of Henry St Clair.

Simon and Tim walked through the park gates and up onto the mound of the former bailey castle. "Is this it?" queried Simon. "It's not much to look at for a three-hour drive is it?" Being a trained archaeologist, Tim was less dismissive of the site. In his mind's eye he could picture the stout timber ramparts that would have been a vital defence for the Norman occupants. He also took in the impressive view down the river towards the sea. That would have been their means of communication with the outside world – and their only safe means of escape, should it become necessary.

He turned to Simon and said "In the 12th Century this was bandit country for the Normans. They needed to maintain coastal communications with Ireland and places like this would have been the outer defences against the armies of the Welsh Princes. It may only be a mound but it's a fascinating piece of history don't you think?" Simon had been driving for over three hours and hadn't been in the frame of mind to think about such things but as Tim spoke he could indeed imagine being in a remote defensive position, far away from your own people, waiting and wondering if an attack would come...

Simon shook himself out of his daydream and said "Let's go back into the village and see if we can get a coffee somewhere. We can do a bit of a recce and see if there's a library or somewhere to get some more information on the castle." They turned the car around and headed back down into the main part of the village. There was a car park with plenty of spaces and a little further on some small cafes. "That looks like a good candidate for some information," said Simon and they sauntered into a building that looked like it had once been a warehouse of some kind. Now it was some sort of arts and tourist information centre but it also served coffee and cake.

They sat down at a table in the tourist centre's cafe and took stock of the situation. "So, we've got a note that suggests the treasure could be in Britain and a coat of arms that suggests it was entrusted to Sir Guy de Bryan. The crest on the van bought us to a place connected with the Sinclair family of Rosslyn Chapel, which is associated with the treasure mythology. Where do we go from here?" asked Simon. Tim didn't have any answers and they were beginning to feel like their journey had been wasted.

Their coffee finished they had a walk around the centre. It didn't hold much in the way of historical information but a helpful member of staff suggested they should visit the County Museum in Carmarthen. "It's probably as good an idea as anything. What do you think?" asked Tim. But Simon had been mulling over the situation and had another idea. "Look it's early yet and we go through Carmarthen on the way home so we can go to the museum this afternoon. Just in case we do happen to find a link between Sinclair and Sir Guy, why don't we follow the river down to the coast and see if it would have been feasible to bring the treasure up river to here?"

Tim could see the logic of the argument and agreed they should press on down to the sea. They returned to the car and dug out an old road atlas. A look at the map showed the river's estuary joined the sea at a place called Laugharne, about four miles away. The road from St Clears passed the remains of the Sinclair castle, over a bridge and swept round to the left to follow the edge of the river valley towards the estuary at Laugharne. The journey was a pleasant run along a decent-sized road flanked by green fields on the rolling hills to either side of the road. Every so often they caught a glimpse of the river they were following from St Clears.

In a short while they found themselves descending a hill into Laugharne. They drove down the hill and passed a few houses and a large impressive Church set back from the road on the left. "Shit! Shit! Shit!" exclaimed Tim "stop the car! Quick!" Luckily no-one was following them because Simon stamped on the brakes and pulled in to the side. "What the Hell's the matter?" he said. "Back up! Back up!" came the excited reply. Simon reversed a short distance to the entrance of the Church car park. "Well bloody Hell! I see what you mean," he said. There, at the entrance to the car park was a sign saying 'St Martin's Church Laugharne warmly welcomes you' and right next to the words was a crest, showing three pillars – heraldic nails – in blue against a background of gold.

"Ha ha!" laughed Tim. "So there is a connection here – and we're in a village right on the coast! Let's go and see what we can find out."

Chapter 10

Simon and Tim drove into the car park of the church and wandered up to the church door. The door was open but the church was empty. "That crest on the sign means there's got to be something here," Tim whispered in the quiet coolness of the Church. "Let's go into the village to see if anyone can help us out." They went back to the car and drove further on into the village.

The road widened out slightly and what appeared to be the main street had wide pavements in front of three-storey houses, suggesting a place of obvious wealth at one time. There was a building with a sign declaring itself to be Brown's Hotel followed shortly by the New Three Mariners Inn. "Look there's a pub, let's go and ask around in there," suggested Simon. A short distance further on there was a small car park, so Simon obligingly found a space and they climbed out of the car to walk back to the pub.

Tim had been observing his friend's new-found enthusiasm with amusement but now he found himself adding to the excitement. Right opposite the car park was a building with a clock tower. He had glanced up to check the time and there, at the top of the dial, was the same symbol of the three nails. "Look at that," he pointed. "That coat of arms is all over the place here."

As they walked the short distance to the pub, Simon moved close to Tim and said quietly "It's probably best not to mention anything about searching for treasure, don't you think? They'd either think we're nuts or – if there is anything to it – we'd be creating some competition." Tim laughed but he could see Simon was serious "OK, we'll be subtle about it," he agreed. They entered the pub, walked up to the bar and ordered a couple of pints. Seeing a menu, they decided they might as well order some lunch while they absorbed the atmosphere.

There were five other customers in the pub: three looked like they'd just come in from working on a building site and two older customers looked like either they had given up work or – perhaps – work had given them up. As Simon and Tim ate their lunch at a leisurely pace, the three builders – or whatever they were – finished their beers and left, presumably to return to their labours. That left the two retired men, slowly drinking their beer and, for the most part, just sitting quietly with only a sporadic burst of conversation.

Simon went up to the bar and ordered a second pint each for him and Tim. "We're visiting the area and saw a blue and yellow shield outside the church and again on the clock tower just down the street. What's the significance of that?" he asked, casually. "I'm not from Laugharne myself," said the barmaid "what can you tell him, Basil?" she nodded towards one of the old customers. "That's the Laugharne coat of arms," the old man replied. "The coat of arms for the village?" queried Simon. "No, boy," corrected Basil. "Don't call Laugharne a village: it's a township." "Oh right" said Simon almost apologetically. "Yes" continued the old man "It's been a township ever since it got its Charter from Sir Guy de Bryan in 1290 or so – and that's his coat of arms you've seen."

Tim wanted to shout out at this latest information but managed to hide his excitement at mention of the de Bryan family. "What do you mean its Charter was granted?" Simon asked the old man. "Well Guy de Bryan, the Lord of the Manor, granted his land and property to the people of the town and the Charter set up Laugharne Corporation to run it." "So who ran the Corporation?" asked Tim. "Oh it still runs today," said Basil. "The men of the town run it: they become a burgess when they get to 21 and the burgesses form the members of the court and choose their own Portreeve to be in charge. The Portreeve is like a mayor – but much older."

"It sounds fascinating," said Tim. "So, are you part of the Corporation?" "Aye, I became a burgess God knows how long ago and I've served on the jury – as part of the court – for about 25 years on and off." "Wow," said Tomo. "That clocktower you mentioned is part of the town hall," said the old man to Simon. "The Corporation meets there every other Monday evening." Simon and Tim thanked the men for their information, bought them each a beer for their trouble and walked out into the sunlight to head back to the car.

"Ah Haa!" said Tim triumphantly. "This sounds promising. All we've got to do is see if the dates tally with the voyage from France and we're in business." "Oh, is that all?" laughed Simon. "This treasure hunting is so easy I'm surprised more people don't do it." Their banter brought them back towards the car and they noticed for the first time what looked like the entrance to a castle, next to a large pink Georgian house. "Let's have a look," suggested Tim. "Why not?" agreed Simon.

They paid their admission fee and entered the preserved remains of Laugharne castle. Tim was thrilled to learn the castle dated from the early 1100s and was in the possession of the de Bryan family at least from the middle of the 13th Century right through to the 14th Century. "The dates are a perfect match," he announced to Simon. The castle was right on the edge of a river estuary and as Tim gazed out from its ramparts towards Carmarthen Bay with the Atlantic ocean beyond, he could just imagine ships laden with Templar treasure making their way towards the little village – sorry, township.

After their tour, the pair returned once again to the car and drove down the hill to an area where the road widened out into a sort of square with a stone cross at its centre. There was another car park by the water's edge at the foot of the castle and they stopped briefly to gain a better view of the castle and its surroundings. The castle faced out towards the estuary of the river they had followed from St Clears and on its landward side was another stream, next to which was a large walled area occupied by what looked like an old house of the Tudor period with a modern bungalow in its grounds. Next to this was the open area with a stone cross.

Both men had a growing feeling that, if the Templar treasure had been brought anywhere, this was the place. The reference to Sir Guy de Bryan matched and unlike Simon and Vicki's visit to the West Country, the dates also matched. Besides, there was no need to haul the treasure any long distance overland because the castle was – or would have been – right on the water's edge.

"Look the time's getting on. If we're going to make it to the museum in Carmarthen before they close we need to get going" said Simon. "OK," agreed Tim and they climbed back into the car to head for Carmarthen and home. What had started as a bit of an anti-climax was turning into something a lot more promising.

Chapter 11

To their satisfaction, Carmarthen museum came up on the BMW's sat nav so Simon pulled out of the car park at the foot of the castle and they set off on the half-hour drive eastwards to their next destination. The museum was housed in the former palace of the Bishop of St David's which, according to Tim's search on his mobile phone, had been the residence of Bishops from 1542 to 1974 and on which site, he noted, a building had existed since about 1290.

The museum had only just reopened after an extensive refurbishment but, being a County museum, it spread its net wide and so despite all the fascinating display there was little specifically about the de Bryan family in Laugharne. One of the displays that caught Tim's attention was to learn of the existence of something called the Black Book of Carmarthen. This was, the display informed visitors, one of the earliest known manuscripts to have been written in Welsh and dated from around 1250. It derived its title of black book purely from the colour of the cover. The collection of poems covers a range of religious and secular topics and includes references to Arthur and Merlin.

Tim was intrigued to learn the name Carmarthen was derived from Cae'r Fyrddin, meaning the place of Myrddin or, in English, Merlin. The Black Book attributes various sayings and prophecies to Merlin and Tim was about to move on when he noticed one of these sayings that made the hairs on the back of his neck stand up. "Look" he whispered to Simon "look at that!" Simon looked where Tim was pointing at the display and read 'Kidwelly was, Carmarthen is, but Laugharne shall be, the Greatest of the Three.' "Calm down old son" said Simon. "We're looking for any logical facts remember. If you start following predictions from mythical wizards God know where we'll end up." It was silly Tim knew, to ascribe any weight to such a phrase, but it encouraged his growing belief that Laugharne really was the resting place for the great treasures of the Knights Templar.

After a largely fruitless search of the museum and with time now running short they headed towards the museum shop and exit. They were about to leave when Simon noticed a book 'The antiquities of Laugharne, Pendine and surrounding areas' by a Mary Curtis and published by the County Council itself. "This might be useful" he said and purchased a copy.

Instead of driving back from Carmarthen to Witney on the same route by which they had come that morning, Simon opted for the easier driving and slightly shorter travel time of the M4 motorway, turning off at Swindon. Fortunately the mid-week early evening traffic was quite light so it was still only around eight-thirty by the time he dropped Tim off at his caravan. It meant he was able to get back to the shop, park the car and be in the flat before nine. "Hi Honey, I'm home" he called as he ascended the stairs. "Hello Darling, have you had a good day?" came the reply. She roused herself from the book she had been reading on the sofa and came over to greet him with a kiss.

Simon related the visit to St Clears castle – or what was left of it – and the discovery of the de Bryan family's castle at a place called Laugharne, right by a river estuary on the coast. "I still don't get the van with the Laugharne crest but a St Clears telephone number" he mused. "Ah, I've solved that one" said Vicki "I've had another look and the 01994 code doesn't just cover St Clears. It includes a handful of other places as well – including Laugharne. I guess that van was from Laugharne all along, you just didn't see it when you were there."

Tim was back in work the following day and had a similar conversation with John Impey. "So does that mean you're going to become a treasure hunter now then Tim?" asked John and they both laughed. "I suppose if you did find the Templar Treasure it would be worth a few quid," said John in a more reflective tone. It wasn't something Tim had considered and he was pretty sure Simon hadn't given the matter much thought either.

Over lunch he began searching for some clue as to the potential value of any such find. The internet was awash with stories and theories about what the missing treasure might be worth. What did become clear was the all-encompassing term treasure needed to be split into two elements. There was the gold and silver currency the Knights would have used in the normal course of their trade and banking operations and then there was a second element: the religious artefacts the Knights had discovered during their occupation of the Temple Mount in Jerusalem.

It was widely accepted the Knights had used their time at the Temple Mount – believed to be the original site of the Temple of Solomon – to tunnel under the mount in search of artefacts. These were no mere obscure artefacts either. These included items such as the Spear of Destiny, the Holy Grail and the Ark of the Covenant – the most famous and most powerful artefact known to the world's great Abrahamic religions of Judaism, Christianity and Islam. Trying to place a monetary value on these relics was absurd but whoever discovered such things would become famous and in archaeology terms would attract the support needed for any project they chose.

He phoned Simon: "Look I think we need to have a chat about our visit to Laugharne yesterday and where we go from here" he said. "Can we meet up?" It was agreed they would meet up in three days time on Sunday afternoon. It was the only time the bookshop and antiques shop were closed together so they could all sit down uninterrupted. "Would you like to stay for dinner?" asked Simon. "Love to" said Tim. "I thought so, I'll let Vicki know" he answered.

Chapter 12

Tim had forgotten he was due to move his caravan to a different site on Sunday. He phoned Simon and Vicki to let them know he would be delayed but by the time he had hooked up the caravan to Florence and decamped to a new site for the next three weeks it was nearly five o' clock before he arrived at Simon and Vicki's flat."Where are you now?" asked Simon as Tim came through the door. "In Kidlington" answered Tim. "It takes a bit longer to come over here but it's much easier getting in to work in Oxford."

The smell of a roast dinner was wafting through from the kitchen but they had time before the food would be ready so they sat down to discuss the 'treasure.' It was Tim that began the conversation: "I know that, up until now, this has been a bit of fun trying to solve a puzzle. But I have been looking into the whole Templar treasure thing and if we found only a tiny fraction of what is supposed to be out there it would be worth a small fortune."

"What kind of small fortune?" asked Simon "Well, based on the current gold price, I calculated a value at just bare metal price," said Tim. Simon could feel his level of interest rising "How much?" he asked. "Er, well – very roughly – and based on a conservative estimate, approximately £90million." "Good Lord!" exclaimed Simon. Vicki was equally shocked and gasped at the idea. "Exactly: it's shocking when you think about it" continued Tim. "My question is, do you agree we might genuinely be on to something and if so is it worth devoting a little more time and money to some exploration?"

Only a fool jumps into such a project without careful consideration and although the idea was exciting Simon and Vicki were cautious in their response. "When you say time and money, what do you mean?" asked Simon. "In the first instance, I think we just need to spend some time in Laugharne if we're serious about this. The money is the cost of staying there," answered Tim. "But how can you be sure the treasure is actually there?" asked Vicki.

"Well there are no guarantees" agreed Tim "but from what we've discovered so far I think the chances of this being the place are much better than fifty fifty." He recapped on the justification for sailing to Britain and the feasibility of sailing around Cornwall and up the Bristol Channel. The person who holds or bears the nails of the Cross had to be the de Bryan family and the dates matched. "Not only that" said Tim "but for me the clincher is the establishment of Laugharne Corporation."

"I'm sorry Tim, but I don't understand the significance of Laugharne Corporation," said Simon. "Did they have a sudden urge for sweeping the roads and street lighting or something?"

"Ha ha!" retorted Tim. "It was nothing like that. Under Norman law, land was granted to noblemen by the king and then the noblemen would grant some of that land to their knights and so on all the way down the social scale. In return the recipient would provide so many men for a set number of days of military service – or the cash equivalent. But when someone died, Norman law required that person's grant of land should pass back up the chain all the way back to the king. "It sounds a bit of a complicated system," observed Vicki. "It was! Completely!" agreed Tim. "It got into a real tangle, with people not knowing who owed what to who."

"So what's this go to do with the Corporation?" Simon asked. "Well, imagine you were looking after something really important and you wanted to keep it safe for all time. You wouldn't want the place where it was hidden being passed to God knows who when you fell off your perch, would you?" "Go on," said Vicki and Simon together. "Well at that time there were only two ways you could ensure land did not revert to someone else. The first was to grant land to the Church – because the Church belonged to God and God is immortal. Or the second was to grant the land to a corporation because, again, a corporation cannot die. The members can come and go but the corporation continues to exist for all time."

A lot of people granted at least some land to the Church because this was seen as a legitimate way of buying your seat in the Kingdom of Heaven when the day came. Although, in this case, I don't think the custody of the Church would have been viewed as entirely trustworthy. The Church was big into the trade in relics at this time remember."

What better than to hide the secret amongst the local population in return for them having their own homes to live in and land on which to farm and feed their families? This would have been a pretty good deal for ordinary people in the early 14th Century – much better than the feudal system in place elsewhere."

This is exactly what the Corporation did. All males became a burgess or member of the Corporation at the age of 21 and they chose the officials and leaders of the Corporation from amongst themselves. They also had shares of land for farming, gathering reeds and so on. The Corporation still operates today and, as far as I can find out, is one of only two such organisations still operating in the UK."

"Ok so you hide the treasure in a place which can never be owned by the king, the Church or any one individual, but what makes you think this Corporation is connected with the Templar treasure?" queried Simon. "Wait 'til you hear this," Tim replied. "The Charter forming the Corporation doesn't have a date on it and some people think it was granted in 1290. But other people's research leads them to suggest the date of the Charter is actually?..." "1307?" offered Vicki. "Absolutely! Yes!" replied Tim with a flourish. "I reckon the ships arrived in Laugharne in 1307. They needed a secure hiding place and they wanted to be sure it was in safe hands for all time. So, simple and most effective safeguard, form a Corporation giving the area to the local population."

"Yes, so why isn't everyone in Laugharne a millionaire, driving around in sports cars?" countered Simon. "Because they don't know it's there," replied Tim. "I think de Bryan and the Templar Knights hid the treasure and then placed the ownership of the land in the hands of the locals who would protect it from outsiders and be content with the Corporation without looking for anything else."

They sat in silence for a while, wondering what to do. Eventually it was Vicki that spoke first "If there really is something there, we would all benefit enormously from finding it," she reasoned. "And if we don't follow it up, I know you'll always be thinking what if," she said, looking at Simon. "Mum and Dad will be back from Canada soon and can look after the shop. I say we spend some time down there and see what we can find out." They agreed: it was time for this idea to become something a little more definite.

Chapter 13

Vicki's parents, James and Mary Dolan, arrived back at London Heathrow from Pearson International, Toronto at 9.15 in the evening. They had left their car with one of the car parking services and had phoned to confirm their arrival with the company so the car would be waiting for them by the time they had collected their luggage. It was a system they had used successfully in the past and meant they were able to drive back to Cheltenham as quickly and easily as possible. They arrived home shortly before 11.30pm so it wasn't until the following afternoon that Vicki was able to call over and see them.

The conversation was along familiar lines "did you have a nice time? How are Jeff and Lyn?" And so on. James Dolan was a Royal Navy Commander who had been stationed at various places in the UK before being posted to Cyprus and then to GCHQ in Cheltenham. Vicki had been sent to Cheltenham Ladies College just before Cmdr Dolan was posted to Cyprus.

Her parents said it was because they wanted her education to be completed in the UK. But Vicki had already realised the secret nature of her father's work and guessed it was because they were worried about her safety. It was a belief that was reinforced when her parents' house in Cyprus had been broken into and ransacked but, instead of reporting the matter to the authorities, her parents had simply tidied up the mess and continued as if nothing had happened.

Vicki had been delighted when her father was posted to Cheltenham although, as a girl in her late teens, she had found it difficult to adjust from being a boarder to being a day girl and living once again with her parents. That was years ago and long before she'd met Simon. Now her parents were both retired – Mary Dolan had worked as a nursery school teacher – and she enjoyed a good relationship with them. Their respectable four-bedroom detached house in Charlton Kings in Cheltenham was far enough away from Witney but not too far that they couldn't visit. When her parents weren't visiting friends abroad or touring Southern Europe they were happy to mind their daughter and son-in-law's shop for them.

"So is that alright? You don't mind?" Vicki was asking. "Of course not Dear," her mother reassured her. It was the same conversation every time Vicki and Simon wanted their help. "Where are you going?" asked her father. "We're going down to West Wales for a few days. We're renting a cottage down there" she answered casually. "That's a strange place for you to be going" said James Dolan. His daughter's holiday locations were usually somewhere hot and sunny like the Mediterranean or Dubai so he was puzzled by this news and a little concerned."Is everything alright between you two?" he asked.

"Yes its fine Daddy, thank you" she said. She hadn't wanted to tell them about their search for the Templar treasure because even she thought it sounded a little odd or embarrassing but she could see if she didn't make a full disclosure to her father he would keep pushing to get to the truth – it had been his job, after all. She told them about the note and their visit to the West Country and how they had discovered Laugharne as being the most likely place to search.

James Dolan thought about it for a while then said "If you're serious about this please be very careful my Darling. People can do strange things when treasure is involved and if you think it might also involve significant religious artefacts, there are all sorts of weirdos who would do anything to get their hands on them." "Oh don't frighten the girl" Mary Dolan chided her husband. "I'm not. I'm just saying be careful who you talk to. Be careful who you trust. That's all." "I will do Daddy, I promise" Vicki reassured him. "Besides, I've got Simon looking after me so I'll be fine." James Dolan had full confidence in his son-in-law, Major Kershaw, but he was still concerned at what they might encounter.

Simon and Vicki had arranged to rent a cottage near Laugharne for the week before the Spring Bank Holiday. There were two reasons for their timing: one it would be quieter because the children would still be in school and so there would be fewer tourists about. The other reason was that cottage rentals increased in price by over 50 percent when the holiday season got under way. They chose a cottage instead of a bed and breakfast or hotel because, as Simon had pointed out, it meant they could spread out maps or drawings and store equipment without attracting any attention.

On the Monday before the bank holiday, with Vicki's parents in charge of the shop, the three adventurers set off for Laugharne. Simon and Tim took the van and Vicki drove the BMW. Simon's training had taught him to take as much resource as possible on an operation – and he had planned this like a military operation. The van contained lights, shovels, ropes and anything else he could think of that might possibly come in handy. The Luton body had no windows and that gave the added advantage of safety from prying eyes for whatever they needed to carry in the back.

Vicki had gone on ahead and collected the keys from the cottage's owner so when Simon and Tim arrived the cottage had been opened up and the heating was on. It was a small stone-built affair with whitewashed walls and a slated roof. More importantly, it was distant from other buildings and people at the end of a short driveway. Inside was a kitchen-diner and sitting room downstairs and two bedrooms and a bathroom upstairs. They had a cup of tea and then set to work on planning their search strategy.

Simon had been able to find a crude plan of the castle as it would have been around the end of the 13th Century, just before the Templars arrived. He unrolled it on the kitchen table and next to it spread out a contemporary large-scale map also showing the castle. They had just started discussing the approach the Templars would have taken and suitable unloading points when the thumb latch on the kitchen door clicked loudly and the door swung wide open.

Chapter 14

The sudden appearance of a stranger in the midst of their discussion made everyone start with surprise. "Hello" said the man. "I'm sorry to make you jump. I just came to see if you were settling in OK?" Simon made to step between the man and the drawings on the table but the stranger had already taken another pace into the room and could see exactly what was on the table. "I'm Carwyn Evans" he announced. "Lucy's husband – you picked up the keys from her earlier?" "Yes, that's right" Vicki answered. "Yes we're all fine thanks" she said and all three smiled politely at Mr Evans.

"Good, good," answered the man nodding his head. "You just down for a holiday then?" he asked. In this part of the world locals still considered it polite and friendly to engage visitors in conversation but to these three visitors with their plans open on the table for him to see, Mr Evans' friendly overtures were less welcome. "Yes, yes that's right" they answered, sounding more evasive than ever.

"Oh, only if you're interested in the castle I might be able to help you out with more information if you want?" he continued. "Well actually" said Simon "we're looking at it as a possible location for a film we're planning. But it's still very confidential so we don't want anyone to know about it yet. You know, we don't want to build up people's hopes if it doesn't actually happen." Mr Evans nodded again "Oh I see" he said. ""We get a lot of people filming in Laugharne so I wouldn't worry about it too much."

After a few more forced pleasantries Mr Evans left – much to the relief of the cottage's three occupants. "We're shooting a film?" Vicki teased Simon. "Well I had to say something" he responded "we were all standing there looking like we'd committed murder or something." Vicki laughed and they turned their attention back to the table – having first made sure the door was bolted. "Ready when you are, Mr Spielberg" Vicki giggled.

Before they had come to Wales, all three had been researching the history of the castle. It was apparent that it had quite a turbulent history in the 12th and 13th Centuries and then underwent further rebuilding and strengthening in the late 13th and early 14th Centuries – just around the time the Templars turned up.

"So, just to be clear, the 1100s and 1200s were turbulent times in this part of the world," said Simon. "That's right," agreed Tim. "The place was subject to constant struggles for control between the native Welsh and the Norman conquerors. As a result the Normans established fortified settlements all along the coast to protect their sea communications with Ireland. Laugharne castle had already been captured and burnt to the ground twice by the Welsh before Guy de Bryan took it over in about 1240. He reinforced it by adding two big round towers and stronger walls but, unfortunately for him, the place was attacked and once again captured by the Welsh in 1258 and de Bryan himself was taken prisoner.

"The first Guy de Bryan died 10 years later in 1268 but his son – also Guy de Bryan – managed to regain possession of the Castle in 1276, eight years after his father's death. Clearly he was in no mood to let the place be taken for a fourth time, so he added another new round tower and a new gatehouse to the inner part of the castle. He also replaced the outer wooden walls with stone. This is how the castle would have been when the Templars arrived in 1307. By that time Laugharne had been peaceful for 30 years or so and it stayed like that right up to the Civil War three centuries later."

Tim continued: "the problem we have is that the castle has been altered several times between then and now, so trying to work out where to look for any treasure hidden in 1307 is virtually impossible. Added to that, the place has been pretty extensively examined by archaeologists and, if anything was left, there's a good chance they would have found it by now."

"Yes I take your point," agreed Simon. "But I don't think we should give up that easily. Have a look at this plan of the Castle as it was in that period and tell me what you think." "What do you mean?" queried Tim "I don't understand." "Well," said Simon. "If you lived in the castle and thought it might be attacked, where would you expect the main attack to come from? If your enemy was likely to be coming from inland it would be against these walls here and here" he said, pointing to the left of the drawing. "If your attackers had managed to breach the outer wall then this area between the outer and inner walls would have had virtually no cover and would have been the killing zone with defenders firing down on them from above."

"Now, while your loyal soldiers were busy fending off the attackers, you would already have prepared contingency plans for escape and that would have meant going out through this wall" – he pointed to the right of the drawing – "into a waiting boat and out to sea." It all seemed obvious thought Tim to himself, when it was explained to you by a trained soldier.

"OK," Simon continued. "So if that over there on the left is where the bad guys are coming in and that is where you're planning to make your withdrawal, where would you be most likely to hide any treasure you didn't want to fall into the wrong hands?" "Somewhere in this area, near your emergency exit," suggested Vicki. "Exactly!" said Simon.

"Now my guess is that if it was important enough – and we're working on that assumption – you wouldn't want to spend ages lugging heavy gold and silver or other precious cargo any great distance to load it into boats, you'd have it ready to ship at a moment's notice." Tim nodded as Simon continued. "I reckon you'd have some sort of tunnel or cave underneath the castle down at sea level where you could load ships without being seen and slip away before anyone was any the wiser."

"But a tunnel like that would have to be well below the ground level inside the castle," said Tim. "How can we have any chance of finding something like that? We can't just stroll up to the Castle staff and ask them if we can dig a few holes please. That would be announcing our search to the whole world and besides; it would take massive resources to do it."

"Well Vicki hasn't seen around the castle yet so why don't we go and have another look around this afternoon," suggested Simon. Accordingly he and Vicki set off, leaving Tim behind reading the book about Laugharne written by Mary Curtis.

Laugharne castle largely consisted of the remains of the main walls and towers. There was little else left except for the magnificent views out over the estuary towards Carmarthen Bay and the open sea. After they had walked around it, Simon and Vicki strolled back down to the car park next to the estuary at the foot of the castle. It was clear what had once been a busy little harbour had silted up over the years and now there was even a footpath that followed round at the base of the castle walls to the Boathouse, the former residence of the famous Welsh poet, Dylan Thomas.

It was now early evening and as the couple walked arm in arm along this grassy footpath they were greeted by the smell of salt and mud that is unmistakably of the sea. The only sound was the haunting song of a curlew out over the salt marshes in the distance.

Simon looked up at the castle walls towering above them. Then he looked down again – and his grip tightened on Vicki's arm. "Look at that" he whispered. "Look at what?" came the reply. "There! Just over behind those bushes" breathed Simon. He couldn't believe no-one else had noticed but there, almost right in front of them a small fall of rock had exposed a vertical fissure that was just wide enough for a man to squeeze through.

"That's almost exactly where I said they would have sited their tunnel" he said. There were still the occasional visitors walking along the path so further exploration would have been impossible without attracting attention. "I think we need to come back here later tonight" said Simon.

Chapter 15

Back at the cottage they excitedly told Tim of their find. They decided it would be best to explore the opening around three in the morning when the area was likely to be at its quietest. In the meantime, their spirits lifted by this fortunate discovery at such an early stage, they decided to pay a visit to the local pub. Although it was within walking distance Vicki drove them there in the car as they would need her to drop them off and collect them later on and there was no sense in being stopped for drink-driving.

The Carpenters Arms seemed a friendly little place and they ordered their drinks and settled down at one of the tables. After a little while a couple of men came into the pub and it was clear from their reception at the bar they were regulars. They got their beers and sat down at a table a short distance away.

"Evening" one of them nodded to the group. "Here on holiday?" he asked. Tim wondered how many times they were going to be asked this same question but here, with nothing to hide, they could be more relaxed. "Yes we're staying up at the little cottage at the foot of the hill" answered Vicki. "Yes, I'd heard that" answered the man. Clearly news travelled fast in this part of the world. "That's Lucy Evans' place," he continued.

"Huh, Lucy's all right but Carwyn, her husband, can be a bit of a funny bugger," chipped in the other man. "What do you mean?" asked Simon. The man explained Carwyn Evans had worked for many years up in London. Nobody knew quite what line of business he'd been in but it was widely thought to have been something not entirely legitimate. Then suddenly he had returned to Laugharne and moved in with Lucy. Overnight the designer suits, gold rings and Porsche sportscar had disappeared and now he lived a quiet life on the farm.

"So he's become a farmer?" asked Vicki. The two men laughed "No, the farmland is all let out to someone else. Carwyn runs his business on the computer" they said. "All I'm saying is, he can be nice as anything and then the next minute he can get really nasty," said the second man.

The conversation between the two tables continued for a little while and then came to a natural conclusion. Simon, Tim and Vicki spent the rest of the evening chatting in that inconsequential way that friends have until the clock moved round towards 11. Then they said good bye to their new friends and their hosts before heading back to the cottage.

Simon immediately settled into one of the easy chairs in the little sitting room for a short nap before they were ready to set out for the castle. It always irked Vicki slightly at how easily he could fall asleep and whenever she'd mentioned it Simon would only laugh and say "Army training Darling." The motto across all the services was, apparently 'eat when you can, sleep when you can and sh*t when you can.' Tim decided to watch a movie on his Ipad and Vicki filled the time by catching up on the novel she was reading.

It was just before three in the morning when Vicki drove Simon and Tim down to the car park at the foot of the castle. All was quiet as Vicki cruised to a stop. There was no moon but the stray light from street lights was enough to see where they were going. Simon kissed Vicki as he and Tim climbed out of the car. "We'll be back in a little while," he said. "If you see anything that looks like it might be a problem, phone me." The two men crossed the small bridge over the stream in front of the castle then followed the grassy path around a slight bend as it followed the path of the main estuary.

Shortly after passing the bend they were out of sight of the car park and hidden from the view of most of the nearby houses. "Here's the opening" whispered Simon to Tim and he pointed a torch shaded with his glove at the rock face. They stepped over a clump of bushes and within moments were sliding themselves sideways through the gap in the rock.

Once they were far enough from the entrance they judged it safe to switch on the lights fastened to their heads. The gap was very tight in places and Simon wished he still had the same waist measurement he'd had ten years ago. Some loose rock had to be pushed downwards so they could get through but then after about ten yards they almost fell into a large chamber. "Bloody Hell – this was a good guess Simon" Tim congratulated him. "We're right under the castle, just about where you said they'd put their treasure."

They began shining their torches around the opening. It seemed the entrance to the cave had been completely closed by a massive rock fall at some point, making it totally inaccessible until the more recent slip at the entrance. It looked like the cave extended further under the castle and they were about to continue their exploration when Tim thought he heard a movement. "Ssh! I thought I heard something" he whispered to Simon. They switched off their lights and stood in the pitch darkness, waiting.

First they heard what sounded like a moan, then they could hear a scraping sound. "Rats?" questioned Tim. It was so dark he couldn't see anything – but he could feel the slight warmth of Simon's breath on his face as Simon spoke: "Fucking big rats," came the whispered reply. Tim wasn't at all sure he liked standing in a cave in total darkness with some unknown thing moving around but Simon's expletive suggested a defiance that was somehow reassuring.

"It's coming from the entrance," whispered Tim. Great, he thought to himself, whatever it is, is between us and our only means of escape. His heart was pounding as whatever it was sounded like it was getting closer. Suddenly there was a scraping sound less than ten feet from him – and the cave was lit by the flame of a cigarette lighter. "Hello again boys" said the owner of the lighter. "Are you planning on filming much in here then?"

Chapter 16

There was no possibility of eluding their visitor so they turned their lights back on and tried to think of a convincing reason for their nocturnal exploration. Simon and Tim looked at Carwyn Evans and after what seemed like an eternity, it was Carwyn who spoke first. It turned out he had been suspicious of the group when he had first met them. "Two men and one woman is an odd party at the best of times" he said "unless they're parents and son. You didn't look like that and the only other explanation might be making a porn film – but you didn't strike me as being here for that either." When he saw the plans on the table his first thought was robbery but, he reasoned, there was nothing of value to steal from the castle. "So that leaves drugs. Are you boys planning on smuggling drugs in Laugharne?" he asked.

Simon looked at Tim, then looked at Carwyn and said coolly "no, we're not drug smugglers – and we haven't broken any criminal laws." Then he added: "who the Hell are you to ask us questions like that?" Carwyn hesitated as if deep in thought. "I'm a copper or rather, I was a copper" he said. "I worked undercover with the drug squad of the Metropolitan Police for six years." He had witnessed some terrible things and had been forced to break the law himself from time to time to maintain his cover.

"In the end I got sick of it" he said. "The rich guys at the top have got the sort of money that buys influence and all we ever did was catch the dregs and wannabe gangsters at the bottom of the pile. I moved back here and tend not to say much about what I did. There are still some nasty people around who would like to pay me a visit."

Simon decided they had no option but to tell Carwyn at least part, of what they were doing. He told him they had found a note suggesting there might be treasure buried at Laugharne castle. "We decided it was worth using our week's holiday to see if we could find out more about it" Simon explained. "Seeing the opening in the rock was just good luck," he added.

"How much do you think this treasure is worth?" asked Carwyn. Simon and Tim looked at each other and Tim said "put it this way, if I'm right we could all be comfortably off for life." "Hmm" said Carwyn thoughtfully. "When you say all of us, would that include me?" They felt they had no option but to agree "besides," whispered Tim "even if it's only a fraction of what we think, it would still be a fortune." Simon nodded in agreement.

"OK, there's four of us but Tim had done a lot of the ground work" said Simon. "How about 40% for me and my wife, 40% for Tim and 20% for you? I think that's generous?" Carwyn considered this for a moment then said "OK let's carry on and see what we can find."

Tim loaned Carwyn a spare torch and together they all moved further into the cave. At the entrance the ground had been firm, presumably due to the fall of rock, but now they found they were struggling through foul-smelling mud slime, sinking up to their shins with every laboured step. "Do you think this would have been a secret tunnel for boats?" mused Tim. "I'm not sure" answered Simon "this slime could have been water at one time but the roof of the cave wouldn't have been high enough for a boat with a mast. I guess it could have been used for rowing boats though."

They squelched their way forward until their lights could pick out the back wall of the cave. To their right they could now make out a low stone-built platform. "So this was a boat dock," said Tim. About halfway along the dock was a doorway and next to it on the dock was what Tim thought at first was a pile of twigs or small branches. He shuddered when he saw a skull and realised he was looking at a human skeleton. It was sitting with legs outstretched and its back against the wall.

They eased themselves out of the mud and stepped onto the dock to survey the scene. It appeared the stone doorway had once held a thick timber door, as the remains of what looked like an oak door adorned with huge metal studs lay about. Inside the doorway to one side was a room about 15 feet wide and perhaps 20 feet deep. The room was empty. Facing the doorway was what looked like stone steps rising upwards but the tunnel served by them had been blocked with large heavy boulders, stone and earth.

The only other feature they could see was another tunnel opening, but this was on the opposite side of the cave to the dock. With nothing else to see, they stepped once more into the ooze and went over to look at this second tunnel. This one was more like a shaft, descending sharply, but it was full of water.

"How did our friend over there get to be stuck in this place" wondered Simon aloud. "If the tunnel behind the doorway was deliberately blocked, why didn't he just swim out of the boat entrance?" Tim had noticed something else lying within the pile of bones. "There were some coins by the body but they're not 14th Century. They're pennies and groats from the 16th Century. I think he's a Tudor."

Carwyn heard the word Tudor and suddenly the second tunnel, the broken door and everything else made sense. "I think I know what happened here" he said. "You thought there might be treasure here from the 14th Century, yes?" Simon and Tim nodded. "I think your Tudor man must have thought so too.

"I don't know if you noticed, but next door to the castle is a Tudor house. The only thing between house and castle is the Corran river. Local rumours always reckoned there was a tunnel from the house to the castle and I think your man might have been one of the people who built that tunnel – and this is it" he said, pointing at the flooded shaft. "I think he might have been looking for the treasure, got as far as here and then his own tunnel got flooded out by the river. He had no way of going back and didn't have the sort of equipment to dig his way out through the rock."

The scenario seemed logical and the most convincing. "If that's true, then there's one other thing we know" said Tim. "There's nothing in that small room, so it looks like there's no treasure." They all looked at each other, digesting the news. Then Carwyn threw back his head and laughed out loud. "Welcome to my world boys" he laughed. "You do all the work and others get the money."

Simon and Tim were quiet and even by the light of the torches looked a little embarrassed. With nothing else to do, the three men started their strength-sapping walk through the mud back to the entrance. Once outside they gulped in their fill of the cool fresh night air. "You've paid for the week" said Carwyn. "You might as well sit back now and relax and enjoy the rest of your holiday." He disappeared into the night, still chuckling to himself.

Simon and Tim got back to the car and tapped on the window, waking Vicki with a start. "Oh my God, you're filthy!" she said as they climbed in. "And you stink as well. Yuk!" "Just take us back to the cottage" said Simon. "We'll have a debrief, a bath – and a whisky."

Chapter 17

"I don't believe it! What a cheeky fucking bastard!" Vicki was furious that Evans had joined Simon and Tim in their search and was freely venting her anger. It was a side of her Tim hadn't seen before and he decided he wouldn't ever want to be on the receiving end of it either. They were back at the cottage having a stiff drink whilst talking over the events of the night.

Simon was being remarkably calm about the whole thing and sought to quell his wife's irritation: "We were wandering around inside an ancient monument after dark. Just being there was probably trespass or something so when he came along we couldn't really do much about it. Either we had to abandon the search there and then and risk him going back to search on his own or invite him along. That way at least he was more likely to keep his mouth shut. Besides we didn't find any treasure so now he thinks we won't be doing any more searching and he'll leave us alone."

Vicki could see the logic of Simon's argument and, having given vent to her feelings, was starting to feel more sanguine about what had happened. There was nothing more to be done that evening, so the two men peeled off their mud-caked overalls and took their turns in the shower while Vicki shoved the dirty clothing into the cottage's washing machine.

They slept in until 10.00 the following morning and after a leisurely breakfast drove the car back into Laugharne to do some sightseeing. In the car park at the foot of the castle they noticed as if for the first time the walled Tudor mansion separated from the castle by only the river in between. Walking along the footpath they used the previous night they noticed, with some discomfort, a trail of muddy footprints leading away from the fissure in the rock and that the bushes near the opening had been trodden down. Simon assured them a good shower of rain would wash away the evidence of their visit and anyway, what did it matter if someone else did find the opening?

Having walked up to the famous poet's boathouse and back, the three sat on a bench and had an ice cream from a local stall. For a while no-one spoke, they just enjoyed their ice cream, the sun on their backs and the smell of fresh air. It was Tim who broke the silence: "So now what?" he asked. "We'd better be going back to work, I suppose," said Vicki. "It's been fun but it's time to get back to the real world." "Hold on just a minute," said Simon. "I don't think our adventure has quite run out of steam just yet." "Oh, nice idea Simon, but I think Vicki's right. I can't see what else we can do," said Tim.

"Well look over there, what do you see?" asked Simon. "A bunch of parked cars?" Tim answered. Simon glared at him but Vicki said "you mean the cross?" "Yes the cross. Now, remember when we were looking through Mary Curtis' book, she mentioned there used to be a monastery here? Somewhere on this square was a monastery and that cross is likely to be the only remaining evidence of its existence." "So what?" said Tim. "Think about it," said Simon. "When the Templars turned up here in 1307 the castle had been trashed three times by the local warlords. If something else kicked off and you had to leave in a hurry you might keep the treasure you could use to buy supplies, weapons and such like nearby. But carrying sacred artefacts like the Holy Grail or the Ark would be a huge liability if you're on the move, especially if you're not familiar with the country." "Go on," nodded Tim.

"If you stored the treasure you needed as spending money in the castle, where better to hide the rest of the treasure and the artefacts than in a nearby religious building? If the castle was overrun, you can bet it would get a pretty thorough going over in the search for arms, treasure etc. But by this stage even the Welsh princes were Christian or if they weren't they'd still respect sacred sites, so a monastery might lose the odd monk but it wouldn't be subject to the same level of search and destroy as a castle. It would be possible – even fitting – for religious artefacts to be hidden in a place of religion and then recovered once again when the bad guys had gone."

"So what do we do?" asked Tim. "Dig up that cross to see what's underneath?" "No, well not yet anyway," said Simon. "Hold on just one minute!" It was Vicki's turn now. "It has been good to come on an adventure together. But I hate the way you had to bargain with Evans last night and that was only because we were doing things in an unauthorised fashion so you couldn't really tell him to get stuffed. If we're going to carry on with this we do things properly. We do our research, work out what or where we want to explore and we ask for the proper permission. No more creeping around in the shadows."

Simon justified their actions by saying what they had done had only been a preliminary investigation but he was quiet when Vicki said "and what would you have done if you had found treasure there last night?" He and Tim agreed that, from now on, they would do things properly, with the proper permissions. "The only problem is," said Tim "that we have no funds. So I guess that's an end to it."

"Not quite," Simon tried to encourage them both. "If we do the research, we might still be able to persuade someone else to invest if we come up with something. At least now we know that others, such as our Tudor friend, think the treasure could be here" he continued. "And we know we need to keep quiet about it until we have something concrete to ask permission for."

Before heading back to the cottage they decided to take a walk around the rest of the little township and get a better feel for the place. Walking up the hill towards the landward entrance of the castle they passed the Tudor mansion and crossed a road bridge over the river. Gazing down at the waters in the gap between the castle wall and mansion wall, Simon paused briefly to offer a thought for the Tudor man who had passed away all those years before, sentenced to a slow death by his watery prison.

At the top of the hill they browsed in the little silversmiths in the lane behind the town hall and then Simon could not resist showing a professional interest in the junk shop a little further along on the main street. There were one or two items of passing interest and while Simon was looking over an old church pew the shop's owner engaged him in conversation. Yes they were here on holiday, no only for the week and staying in a cottage, yes the one owned by Lucy Evans. Then Simon asked: "Do you have any information about Laugharne Corporation?" The man introduced himself as Michael Heath and offered him a copy of the book by Mary Curtis but Simon already had a copy and so declined. Then Heath had an inspiration and disappeared into his office.

He reappeared a moment or two later holding a slim white publication. "This is probably the most useful book for you" he said. Simon looked at the booklet. It was called simply 'Laugharne Corporation' written by EV Williams MA, Jesus College, Oxford. "Mr Williams was the church warden in Laugharne in the 1940s and 50s" explained Heath. "He probably knew more about the Corporation than anyone and I don't think you'll find a more detailed history of it anywhere else."

The booklet was an original and quite hard to come by, explained Heath so they negotiated a price and Simon paid the man and stepped from the dimly lit shop into the sunlight to meet the other two waiting outside. They decided to head back to the cottage and see what more information they could glean from their books, maps and the internet.

Chapter 18

Philippe de Chretien had managed to bring his convoy of ships with their priceless cargo safely to harbour in Laugharne and after meeting with his old comrade he felt able to relax, albeit not fully. He and his itinerary had been treated to a fine meal by their hosts on the evening of their arrival and now, after a good sleep in a bed that did not pitch and roll with the sea, he felt reinvigorated and ready to complete his duty.

"Our needs are twofold," he began explaining to Guy after they had breakfasted. "First, there is our treasury of gold and silver that we use to carry out our work. This is already in strong chests and can be moved to any secure place. The second is of far greater importance than mere earthly riches" he paused and glanced around. "It is the Holy relics of which I spoke yesterday. We have the very cup from which our Lord drank at the Last Supper and which held his blood at the crucifixion. We also have the Ark of the Covenant." Guy looked startled: "you mean the very ark that contains the words of God, given to Moses?" "Yes."

For a moment or two Guy did not speak. Like his father he was a man of deep religious conviction. He knew some of the 'relics' that were venerated in churches and monasteries or hawked around the markets were mere invention intended to profit their keepers but this, this was different. His father had impressed upon him how the true Knights Templar were men of deep religious faith and now, here in front of him, this Knight claimed stewardship of one of the most important items of faith in the whole world.

Almost afraid to ask the question, he leaned forward and said: "the Ark is said to actually show the power of God. Can you be sure this is the true Ark and not a device to fool the innocent out of their money?" Philippe understood his host's concern but was able to answer the question with complete conviction and honesty. "I have seen with my own eyes the Ark show its power" he replied. "Men who have tried to lay hands upon it have been thrown across the chamber by lightning. It makes a sound like the beating of many wings when it is approached and only Knights Templar in their full uniform of mail and tabard with cross can touch it without harm. Even then their bodies are bathed in the light of God. It can only be carried between two poles of wood if one is to avoid the terrible wrath of God."

Guy was awestruck. "Can I see it for myself?" "Certainly you can. But you will understand we cannot make its presence here widely known. I ask that you consider very carefully before letting even the most trusted members of this house know what is in our care." Guy understood Philippe's concerns. He knew that whoever possesses the Ark holds tremendous power. The stewards of the Ark have a duty and responsibility to ensure it is never taken and used for anything other than to perform the will of God. But to many men the riches they might make for themselves simply by passing on the Ark to others would be an irresistible temptation.

"Where would you conceal such a treasure?" Guy asked. "We are beginning to strengthen the defences of this castle and could build a secret place that would be worthy of such Holy things." "Thank you for your generosity," said Philippe. "We would indeed wish to keep our gold and silver close at hand and my fellow Knights have much experience they can bring to building concealments within and below these walls. But I would respectfully ask that the relics are enclosed elsewhere.

"We have made the mistake in times past of sequestering them in strongholds connected with our order. But if matters should turn against us we know our foes will search every smallest place to find these things and we are left with no choice but to remove them and go elsewhere in haste. We thought they were safe in France but now King Phillip has turned against us we have escaped with them by only the smallest of margins. This time they must be hid where our enemies – and even those who presently are our friends – would not think to look."

"I understand your predicament," Guy replied. So where would you have us hide them? We can take them to caves along the coast or perhaps to a secret place in the woods hereabouts?" "I have given much thought to this" confessed Philippe. "The place must be clean and dry as is fitting for such precious treasures. So I do not think a cave or the woods are suitable. Also, they should be within the sound of people praising God and giving Thanks."

Philippe continued: "I will have discharged my sacred duty therefore if we were able to keep them for all time on Holy Ground; hidden in a place where they would not decay, and where they would be truly safe from the avarice and greed of men." Guy considered Philippe's words carefully. At last he said "there are many Holy places hereabouts but if the relics must be transported without witness then the nearest Holy place is just over there," he pointed to the monastery just a few feet from the castle walls.

"That sounds like a worthy proposition," agreed Philippe. "Does the Father Abbott have your absolute trust?" The place was right as it had no connection with the castle or the Knights Templar and it was Holy ground... and yet he could not be sure how the Father might respond to such a request. "Your hesitation says much," observed Philippe. "I suggest we approach the Father Abbott with great circumspection to see what he might be minded to do."

Chapter 19

Father Ridolphus was content with his life in Laugharne. Being quite a busy little port, many sailors came to give thanks for safe deliverance after their voyages. The Flemish merchants and weavers prospered in times of peace and they too came to pray and give thanks. Even the poor gave what they could but often the thanks was for the more practical work of the monks in ministering to the sick and infirm. They all hoped that, one day, they might enter the Kingdom of Heaven but in the meantime they would try their best to stave off that day for as long as possible.

The Abbott had come originally from Italy many years past and through the power of God and the direction of the Holy Roman Father he had ended up in the land of the Cymrics, as the leader of this Cistercian order. The Lord de Bryan was of a similar age to him and he had discovered the Lord Guy had travelled through his home country on his journeys to and from the Crusades. He knew many of the towns and cities of Ridolphus' youth and shared a love of the cuisine of that country. Over the years the two had become good friends.

He was sad his friend had been taken ill and he had sent his best physician to tend to him. Now he was on his way the short distance across the square, known to all simply as Y Grist (in English the Christ) to see his friend for himself. Although Lord de Bryan's arm still hung limp and almost lifeless by his side, he had regained some power of speech. "Ridolhus 'ay hrend," he said as the Abbott entered. The Abbott could see his eyes light up at his arrival and he embraced the man warmly. Their conversation was limited and Ridolphus was anxious not to tax his friend too greatly but as he was leaving, Lord Guy said "meet 'ay hrend Hilippe. Ee aas a Hrusader hike me."

Ridolphus struggled to understand his friend but as he left the chamber he met the younger Guy. They exchanged pleasantries and discussed Lord Guy's health. "They say he is slightly improved" said Ridolphus and Guy was able to confirm that yes, that was indeed true. "I will continue to pray for him" said the Abbott. Then Guy said "Father Abbott I would like you to meet a friend of my father's. They went on the Crusades together." Philippe stepped forward and bowed to the cleric.

"What brings you to our township?" asked the Abbott. It was a perfectly reasonable question. Guy began to say "he is a Knight..." when Philippe cut in and said casually "I was a Knight a while ago and wanted to meet up with my old friend one last time before we both stand before our Maker." "It looks as if God was guiding you my son" said the Abbott. "I worry that the Lord Guy may be closer to meeting his Maker than either of us and the time draws near for me to administer the last rites." Philippe nodded and they exchanged a sombre look at the plight of their mutual friend.

After the Abbott had departed Philippe apologised to his host for interrupting him. "I am sorry Guy. I would like to know this man better before we share the details of my mission with him. I cannot risk the security of the Ark but I think I may have a way to test the loyalty of the Abbott."

As the days drew on, Philippe's fellow Knights continued to guard their precious cargo on the ships moored in the harbour. They took turns on the ships and always lay ready with arms nearby in case any disaster should befall them. Philippe made a point of speaking with the Abbott whenever he encountered him. Sometimes this was during visits to the Lord Guy but more often it was just after prayers in the monastery chapel. Ridolphus was impressed at the devotion of this friend of Lord Guy.

One evening after the Abbot had dined in the castle, Philippe took him to one side. "Father Abbott, you are a man of God, do you believe in miracles?" Ridolphus looked at him with curiosity "I do believe in the power of God to perform miracles yes" he said. "Father Abbott I have prayed in your chapel for my friend to recover but I believe it is the power of a Holy relic in my possession that has done much to restore his health. Can I now entrust it to you for safekeeping?"

"Of course my son, where is the relic?" "Before I give it to you, will you make the same promise that I made, that you will not reveal your possession of it to more people than is necessary and that you will never use it for personal gain or adulation?" The Knight's request seemed unusual but understandable, given the trade in Holy relics of all kinds. "You have my promise," agreed the Abbott. "I will bring it to you on the morrow" said Philippe.

True to his word, Philippe called on the Abbott the following day, after morning prayers had finished. Guy had accompanied him. They sat facing Ridolphus over a simple table and Philippe reached down into his bag and withdrew an object carefully wrapped in linen. "This is the relic that has restored Guy's father, the Lord de Bryan, thus far" he said. As he unwrapped it, he said to the Abbott "my gift to you is the cup of Christ." Guy had not seen it beforehand and both he and the Abbott stared in awe at the small wooden goblet. It was battered and clearly of great age and inside it appeared the wood was stained with wine... or perhaps even blood.

Ridolphus crossed himself and said to Philippe "where did you get this?" "It was entrusted to me after my return from the Holy land" he answered truthfully. "Why would you receive it? Such a thing if it were real would not have been entrusted to an ordinary Knight? Before I take this, I insist you tell me the truth."

Philippe confessed that he was a Knight of the Templar Order, that he managed to gain passage across the sea to escape from persecution by the King of France and that he sought a place of safety for this Holy relic. What he said was true without revealing more than was absolutely necessary. Ships arriving from Flanders were a common enough sight in Laugharne due to the trade of the Flemish merchants and weavers so did not arouse the suspicion of the Abbott.

"I have heard news that King Phillip is trying Templar Knights for heresy" said the Abbott at last. If you are a Templar then my duty to the Church is to give you up to be tried for heresy. But you are also a good friend of my friend and I have witnessed your devotion to him and to your worship of God. If I accept this relic into my care I must decide how to best to do what is right before God."

Almost involuntarily, Philippe found himself gripping the dagger he had hidden under his tunic. The Abbott said "I believe I must accept the cup and I will honour the promise made to you about its keeping. But as to what my duty is towards you, I shall have to pray for guidance. In the meantime, go in peace my sons." Philippe's hand relaxed on the dagger. He and Guy stepped out of the monastery into the frosty sunshine of the late autumn day and walked back to the safety of the castle.

Chapter 20

Guy had not been privy beforehand to Philippe's plan and was astonished by what he had just witnessed. "You gave away the cup of Christ! The Holy Grail!" he exclaimed to Philippe. "I did not give it away," Philippe answered calmly and quietly. "I entrusted its safekeeping to a man of God. I believe he will keep his promise and not reveal it or treat it casually but I also need to know what he will do next. Now he has knowledge of who we are it will not tax him to work out that we may have treasure with us. This will tell me whether he is absolute in his obedience to Rome – in which case we may have to flee or be arrested for heresy – or whether he uses his own judgement. If it is the latter then perhaps he may help us further in our mission."

The strain of the past few weeks and the heavy responsibility he bore was beginning to take its toll on Philippe. He had left his home with only sufficient time to take the barest essentials. He had organised the removal and clandestine transport of some of the most important treasures of his Order and brought them safely across the sea to another country. Now he had rekindled an old alliance and forged new but all the time he was thinking and planning for the safe refuge of his precious cargo. At his time of life he should be starting to ease into his retirement not running such an important mission. He was tired and slumped into a chair in his chamber as he awaited the reaction of the Abbott.

Guy was also pondering the situation. It was but a short while ago he had been busy looking at drawings with his father and instructing the masons and carpenters on works to strengthen the castle defences and increase its accommodation. That work had now all but taken on a life of its own and was continuing under the supervision of the master craftsmen. Then his father had been taken ill and although their prayers and the attentions of Brother Jerome had seen some improvement in his father's health he could not help but feel his days were numbered. That would mean he would become Lord and fully take on all the responsibilities entailed in the role.

Added to this was the arrival of these Knights, the arrival of their treasure and the arrival of the most important relic of the Christian world. On the strength of his father's friendship with Philippe de Chretien he had promised to provide any assistance they may need and while he felt no desire to renege on that promise he was anxious about what it may demand. If the arrests for alleged heresy spread from France to Britain, might he have to hide the Knights, fight alongside them or even risk arrest himself? There was no purpose in trying to foretell what may happen, he told himself. He would follow the example of his father's friend and see what the Abbott chose to do.

As he gazed out over the river, looking towards the ocean beyond, there was a flurry of hurried footsteps and some muffled shouts. "Come quickly my Lord, it is your father," said a servant. Guy ran to his father's chamber and was followed shortly by Philippe and all the other members of the household. Guy de Bryan, Knight Crusader and Lord of Laugharne, lay dead. "He had another apoplexy and passed before I could get help" said the nurse, a mature woman and long-time trusted servant of the household. She was close to tears at the loss of her master but also fearful she might be punished for not having saved him. "It is well, thank you, Martha" said Guy quietly "you may leave us now" he added and grasped her hand in affection. Unable to control herself any longer the woman burst silently into tears and fled the room.

"Bernard, fetch the Father Abbott please" Philippe ordered his squire. Then he stood back waiting on Guy before he could come forward and kneel to pay his own respects to his dear departed friend. Guy had been expecting his father's death and the household had begun to prepare for it but he was still overcome now that it had happened. "Will you all please leave us" he instructed. The little group quietly withdrew; Philippe standing guard outside the door. Alone with his father, Guy knelt at his side. He brushed the man's cheek with his hand and then held his father's hand. It was a large, strong hand already beginning to grow cold. Guy could feel the tears rolling down his cheeks at his loss.

His father had been his guide, his mentor in all things. He had shown him how to administer the township with justice and fairness. He had shown him how to fight, how to plan for battle but also how to construct buildings for peace as well as war. Although they had never spoken of such things, he had truly loved him.

Guy recovered himself and invited Philippe back into the chamber. Philippe also felt the loss of his friend, perhaps more deeply than people would know. They had fought side by side in the Holy land, sometimes to a standstill. When the fighting stopped they had stood together, silent save for the pounding of their hearts and the gasping of their lungs for air. Muscles turned to jelly, sweat pouring through their clothes and down their faces, mouths dry as parchment, with the stench of blood in their nostrils and its metallic taste on their tongues. They had saved each other's lives many times over in encounters such as that and it had created a bond between them that no-one else could possibly comprehend.

Philippe had seen more dead bodies in his lifetime than he cared to remember. Most of them, apart from the dreams, meant nothing to him but this was his friend. He felt the loss a deeply as Guy but it was important not to let it show.

Father Ridolphus arrived, crossed himself, prayed for his deceased friend and tendered his sympathies to Guy and Philippe. He stayed for a while both as a mark of respect and out of a genuine sadness for the loss of his friend and then he returned to the monastery. He realised the death of his friend had determined what he would do regarding his dilemma.

Chapter 21

Since arriving in Laugharne the previous day, Simon, Vicki and Tim had been on a rollercoaster of emotions. The thrill of unexpectedly finding the cave then, for Tim at least, the shocks of being discovered and making a gruesome discovery and then the disappointment of not finding anything. This plus the lack of uninterrupted sleep meant none felt too inclined to do much on their return to the cottage. It was around four o' clock when someone suggested a visit to nearby Pendine Sands for a walk along the beach in the last few hours of the spring daylight.

The decision was a good one: At this time of year there was hardly anyone about in the little seaside holiday resort. They walked down onto the beach of golden sand and stared eastwards back towards the direction of Laugharne. The sands stretched for seven miles or so until they met the river estuary at Laugharne and such a great expanse had brought the place fame as a venue for motor speed events, most notably in the 1920s and 30s with the likes of Parry-Thomas and Malcolm Campbell.

Today the vast open space was a place for the three visitors to free their minds from their immediate concerns and take time to reflect on their aims and priorities. There was no doubt they had each in their own way been taken up with the idea of finding lost treasure – and not just any lost treasure – but the famed Templar treasure that had grown a mythology all of its own. But after the events of the previous 24 hours their almost child-like enthusiasm was growing into a more mature, professional approach to searching for a prize of worldwide fame.

Enthusiasm for the project had waned earlier in the day back at the cottage, but after a supper of fish and chips on the seafront whilst watching a sunset that changed from pale blue to almost white and then baby pink they felt ready to look again at the steadily growing pile of research material they had accumulated. It was Tim who reignited their flame of interest in the subject. "I've been looking at the Curtis book again" he said "and comparing it with other texts. Her description of the monastery is pretty detailed yet other sources either ignore it or suggest it never existed in the first place."

"Surely history is full of anomalies like that" said Simon. "Well yes," Tim answered. "But you've read her description, you saw the cross that is still there and even the name of the site – the Grist, or in English the Christ – tells you it existed. My point is, why would other people try to deny the monastery ever existed unless" – "unless they were trying to hide something!" interrupted Simon. "Yes I see what you mean."

Treasure hunters, researchers and investigators always look for clues but, as Simon knew from experience, creating subtle doubts or sometimes even flat out denial, could be surprisingly effective in persuading them to discard the evidence. "I said they would have looked to hide the relics in a religious site" he said. "So I think you could well be on to something." Tim showed Simon and Vicki a 14th Century text that described Laugharne yet failed to make any mention of its monastery and the book about Laugharne Corporation Simon had bought that afternoon also again cast doubt on its existence.

"Do you think the relics could actually be buried under the cross on the Grist? asked Tim. "Well it did occur to me" Simon admitted. "But you know that cross doesn't originate from the 14th Century don't you?" "No it's a replacement for the original, I accept that" agreed Tim. "But if you look at the customs of Laugharne that cross has been involved in ceremonies of all sorts since way back when. It's very likely to originally have been a Saxon preaching cross – there's another one in the churchyard of Llansadurnen, just three miles off to the west."

"That square is still a big area," said Simon. "We'd need to see if we can find any more details of the monastery's exact site before we can do anything else. With their interest piqued at the thought of a mediaeval cover up, they resumed their researches with a new vigour.

Vicki took the opportunity to check her emails and then called her parents to see how they were getting on in the shop. They'd had a good day and sold several items they said. "Are you making progress with your search?" asked James Dolan. Vicki gave a limited report on what they had been doing, omitting altogether any mention of the visit to the cave and finished off by saying they had been to Pendine Sands. "Pendine?" said her father. "I've been there a while ago – there's an MOD experimental range behind the dunes along the beach." "Er yes that's right Daddy," replied Vicki, trying to hide her lack of interest. Her father hadn't missed the change in tone and laughed. "OK I'll leave you to it Darling" he said.

Her phone call finished, Vicki was still sitting with her laptop open in front of her so she decided to see if anyone had connected relics like the grail or the ark to Wales. To her surprise there was a result that claimed the Holy Grail was kept in a bank vault in Aberystwyth. She searched further and found a photograph of the cup and an explanation of its history.

The cup had come from the Cistercian monastery at Strata Florida in mid Wales, about 60 miles north of Laugharne. It was claimed the cup had been given to the monks by Joseph of Arimethea and had remained in the monastery until it was passed to the owners of Nanteos Mansion for safekeeping during the dissolution of the monasteries in the reign of Henry VIII.

"Guys come and have a look at this" she said excitedly to show them what she'd found. "So these people claim the grail came from the monastery at Strata Florida?" said Simon. "Yes that's right" said Vicki. "Sorry Honey, but how does that help us?" "Well," Vicki continued "If you look at when the monastery in Strata Florida was founded... and then you look at when the monastery in Laugharne ceased to exist..." "Don't tell me," said Tim "they're the same date, right?" "Well not exactly, but pretty close" said Vicki.

"So you two think the relics were in the monastery in Laugharne and then for some reason they were moved to a different monastery?" asked Simon. "It sounds plausible, don't you think?" replied Vicki. "Yes I bloody do" agreed Simon. "Well, where does that leave our search?" asked Tim. "Hmm" said Simon "I guess it means we don't have to try and dig up a car park in Laugharne any more – thank goodness. Although I don't know how we'd have done that anyway. I'd love to know why they moved the treasure out of Laugharne though," he added thoughtfully.

"Well perhaps they didn't move all of it, or perhaps they dispersed it around the place to make it harder to find" said Tim. The puzzle of a monastery whose very existence seemed to have been covered up was intriguing. It was made more so by the thought that a cup claimed as the Holy Grail could conceivably have come from this very same monastery. And Tim's suggestion that the treasure had been hidden in more than one place was looking more plausible than ever. It was with these thoughts turning over in their heads that they agreed to leave the next step in their researches until the following morning.

Chapter 22

Ever since Philippe had revealed himself to be a Templar Knight, Ridolphus had struggled with his conscience in trying to decide the right thing to do. He knew that heresy was often misused as an excuse to arrest political opponents and from what he knew this was the likely situation in France between King Phillip and the Templars. But some of the stories of what they were accused of were beginning to reach even this corner of the world and they were quite shocking.

If he, Ridolphus, suspected anyone of heresy it was his clear duty to have them arrested and tried. And yet... he could find nothing to suggest Philippe was a heretic and he was reluctant to have him and his fellows arrested merely on baseless rumours. Further, if any arrests were made it was likely his good friend's son, Guy, might also become caught up in the process and tried for heresy.

If anyone should come looking for these Knights and it became known that he and members of his monastery were aware, or even suspected, Guy's friends of being Knights Templar then the consequences could be serious for them also. He had begun to form a plan in his mind and now that his close friend and ally, Lord de Bryan, had passed away it clarified the situation and strengthened his resolve to do what must be done.

Ridolphus requested to meet again with Guy and Philippe. Word came back from the castle that they were unable to attend him in the monastery but they would be honoured to receive him in the castle after he had finished evening prayer. This was Philippe's idea. If Ridolphus planned to have him and his fellow Knights arrested then he would despatch him and, under cover of darkness, make for the open sea.

They met in the Great Hall and sat close together in front of a strong fire. The winter weather had begun to take a hold now and cold, damp winds eddied around both outside – and inside – the castle walls. As they warmed themselves by the dancing light of the flames, Ridolphus spoke first. "I must apologise, for when last we met I was suffering from a severe cold. It had affected my hearing and I did not catch some of what you might have said. I am however, in your debt for bestowing upon me the honour of stewardship of such a Holy relic.

"For some time now I have felt that God has been calling me to continue my work in another place. I believe the gift you have bestowed, followed so closely by the passing of my dear friend, are indisputable signs that this is the case and that now is the time for me to move on. I will therefore be removing the monastery and taking my brother monks with me to a newly-formed monastery far to the north of here. Brother Jerome will stay here to minister to the sick in the hospital but you may find the stone and materials of the remainder of the monastery of use in building perhaps a new chapel or other consecrated building here in Talacharn."

"Father Abbott, you are indeed a good man and a man of God" said Philippe. I am disappointed you will be leaving Talacharn as I had hoped to work with you, but I understand your calling to another place." "Indeed so," agreed Guy "we wish you goodness in your new monastery."

"Before you depart Talacharn, can I ask that you be the one to conduct the funeral of my father?" "Of course, it will be my honour to do so," answered Ridolphus. "Where will he be buried?" This was a question that, until moments ago, had not been in doubt. Guy had always thought his father would be buried in the chapel of the monastery, within sight of the castle. Now, if the monastery was no longer going to be there, he would need somewhere else to be laid to rest.

"There is the Church at Llansadurnen" said Guy "it enjoys fine views over the bay of Caerfyrddin. Or we could consecrate ground here within the castle walls." "If I may be so bold," said Ridolphus "I think your father had once said he did not wish to be buried where the blood of men had been spilt in anger." "Yes, that is true" agreed Guy. "Where would you suggest, Father Abbott?" "Perhaps you have forgotten" answered Ridolphus "there is a small church not far from here that sits amongst the trees. It is a Saxon church on a place that was Holy both to the Romans and the Druids before that. Your father was a good and just man. Perhaps it would be fitting to rebuild the church and lay him to rest there?"

"Of course" Guy answered. "That would be the perfect place. We will survey it on the morrow and make it a place worthy to the memory of my father."

Ridolphus arose to leave and both Guy and Philippe took his hand and shook it warmly. Ridolphus and Philippe looked into each other's eyes and both knew and understood the other. Guy was also aware of the upheaval and sacrifice Ridolphus was making. It was almost certainly due to the friendship he had enjoyed with Guy's father but, thought Guy; it may also be due at least in part to a respect he had found for Philippe.

Philippe had commanded his Knights to be ready in case the evening had ended in flight, so he was greatly relieved this had not transpired. But he had not expected the Father Abbott to take the courageous course of leaving Talacharn and diplomatically putting as much distance between the monks and Knights as possible. If fortune turned even further against the Templars, then the innocence of the monks would be assured and they could not be implicated or involved in what might happen.

The problem now lay in where to hide the Holy relics in Philippe's charge. He had thought the monastery would have been a fitting place but now it was to be dismantled and the site deconsecrated. On reflection, he now realised the Father Abbott would never have allowed them to build a suitable repository – and he was too clever for them to have built it without his knowledge.

Chapter 23

Later that day, in accordance with established custom and practice, Guy washed his father's body in water as part of the process of purification to ensure passage into heaven. Philippe came to him and said "my fellow Knights have experience of preparing the dead and we would be honoured to embalm Sir Guy that people may have opportunity to see him and pay their respects."

Guy agreed and the Knights set about their sacred task. First he was washed again, this time with the best white wine from the castle. Then quicksilver was procured and poured into the ears, nostrils and mouth. Finally a mixture of sweet-smelling herbs and incense was placed in the body and stopped up with oakum.

The carpenter, Pedr Ifans, had been working on the castle and was now sent to make a coffin from the boards of elm he kept in his workshop. Most people of the township could ill afford a coffin and instead were buried in just a shroud. Those with some wealth were laid to rest in a simple wooden coffin but for Sir Guy the coffin would be adorned with fittings of silver and gold as befitted his status.

Whilst the coffin was being made and the arrangements for the funeral set in hand, the body, wrapped in a shroud save for the face, was displayed in the castle that people might come and pay their respects. For six days they came, everyone from the lowliest in the town to the merchants and the monks and nobles from as far away as Caerfyrddin and Penfro. They paid their respects in Welsh, Flemish, Norman-French and Latin.

Some time after midday Guy and Philippe set out along King Street, named in honour of the visit to the town by King Henry II in 1172, and made their way to the little mound set in a grove of oaks that had been a sacred place since before Roman times and was now a Saxon Church. The Church was a modest affair, built of strong blue limestone from the quarry at Coygen but roofed with slate from Cilgerran rather than thatched with reed from the Corran as was more common in this area. It comprised of a small porch leading into the nave, which was a bare room some 20 feet across and 30 feet long. At the eastern end there was no chancel for choir or priests, just a single step up into a sanctuary in which stood a wooden altar covered in a simple linen cloth. The only decoration was a stone carved effigy of a woman, set into one wall and probably a vestige of the original Roman temple.

The reaction of the two men was quite different: Philippe loved its simplicity and thought to himself what a good place to be laid to rest. The younger man was upset. He felt himself embarrassed that after all his father's labours in encouraging peace, prosperity and justice in the town, he should not be in such a lowly place. "This is truly a place where a man could be at peace," observed Philippe. "But it seems little reward for a man who devoted his life first to the Crusades and then to the peace and prosperity of this town" said Guy.

"Well, our Lord was no stranger to humble surroundings" countered the older man. "Yes I know, but his word is passed on to us in the Scriptures. "There is none to pass on the word of my father's works and in such a simple place as this he will surely not be thought of in high regard. I am afeared that in a generation his memory will be lost."

It was then that Philippe had his epiphany: "Of course!" he exclaimed and fell to his knees in front of the altar to give thanks. When he had finished he turned to Guy and explained. "I believe we have been guided to this path by God. Your wish and my mission are to be fulfilled together. I believe we will lay your father to rest in this place but he has one last eternal role set out for him. He will guard the relics we have brought and protect them from harm in this very place.

"We will build a new church. It will have the majesty deserved of the place that houses the ark of God's Covenant. Yet the presence of your father will protect it from the inquisitive or the evil-doer." Guy was humbled at this news. It would please his father to be forever in the service of the Lord and it would become a fitting shrine to the man who had in his own way devoted his life to suit and service of God.

"But how shall we undertake the work?" questioned Guy. "We cannot build a church to house the ark without attracting attention." "Do not be troubled, we have skilled engineers in our party" said Philippe. "They learned their craft, building and tunnelling in the Holy land itself. As for keeping the ark a secret, I believe the Lord has shown us this place and the Lord will help us in our endeavours." Philippe was almost ecstatic at his revelation from God. After months of worry, he believed this was the chosen way forward and his mood would brook no obstacles.

For his part Guy was sad at the loss of his father but felt reassured the role that had been set for him in the little Saxon church would surely guarantee his entry into the kingdom of heaven. The paths of the Father Abbott and Philippe were now set and even he began to feel a certain calmness. The two men walked back to the castle, past the houses of the wealthy merchants, both silent, absorbed in their own thoughts. Lights began to flicker in the growing dusk and as they reached the castle gate stars were already twinkling in the winter sky.

Suddenly, a brilliant shooting star caught their vision as it sped across the sky. "Surely a sign from God," said Philippe and Guy nodded. "Happy St Andrews Day," he said "In three days hence it will be Advent: the beginning of the new Christian year and, perhaps, the beginning of a new year for us."

Chapter 24

The funeral was held on a Tuesday, six days after Sir Guy's death. The coffin, resplendent in all its gold and silver decoration, was lifted on to the shoulders of six men including the new Lord Guy de Bryan and brought from the castle along King Street in procession to the church. This was a rare occasion in that the fishermen, cockle pickers, publicans, sailors and labourers and all others living in the lower town ventured en-masse into upper town, which was the preserve of the wealthier artisans, traders and merchants.

All were united in paying their respects as the Lord had been a just man, helping those in need and protecting those in danger. Some attributed his compassion to weakness or thought he had been touched by madness, but people who had known him as a younger man knew it was his experiences in the Crusades that formed his character. His compassion came from a position of strength, not weakness. As the procession passed, people fell in behind the coffin and followed it towards the church.

It was a bitterly cold day but that had not stopped almost the entire town from attending. At points along the way the pall bearers paused and their places under the heavy coffin were taken by others. All except Guy: he would bear his father all the way from castle to church. The procession reached the tiny church and brought the coffin to rest before the altar. As it was the beginning of the Christian year, anticipating the birth of Christ, it was not appropriate for the church to be brightly decorated – nor indeed would it have been easily achieved, given the lack of flowers in winter. But despite this, the wreaths of holly and hangings of ivy had a pleasing appearance in the candle light.

The mass was conducted in Latin but Philippe and his Knights were surprised to also hear many chants, hymns and songs in Welsh and Flemish. At the end of the service Lord Guy stepped outside the church and addressed the vast crowd outside. He thanked them for their kindness and then announced "Let it be known to all the innkeepers and hostelries of the town that all drink consumed this day shall be the gift of the Lord de Bryan to the people of Talacharn."

A cheer went up and the people dispersed to begin, in earnest, their wake in honour of the nobleman. "Father Abbott, please join us in the castle" Guy invited. "I will be pleased to do so" he replied. With that Guy, Philippe and Ridolphus set off for the castle by way of every inn and hostelry so they might arrange payment to the keepers of every one. It was late when they eventually returned to the castle and none were too steady on their feet, but the sounds of laughter and singing that floated heavenwards from all parts of the town assured them that the spirit of the Lord Guy de Bryan was being honoured.

The days that followed saw much activity in the little town. With the ceremony around Lord de Bryan's funeral now passed, bemused monks began in earnest to prepare for the move to their new monastery at Strata Florida. They carefully packed precious Communion sets of chalice, ciborium and paten for administering the Eucharist and stowed their precious parts of the true cross in a sturdy reliquary. True to his promise, Ridolphus told no-one of the relic entrusted to his personal care.

At the same time, the friends of Sir Guy were labouring to build a new centre of Divine worship at the other end of the town on the site of the old Saxon church where the former Lord now lay. Townspeople had much to gossip about: it was, they agreed, a strange coincidence 'their' monks were leaving as the new church was being constructed. Why hadn't the Lord de Bryan been laid to rest in the monastery? Or the small chapel in the castle itself?

The majority of ordinary citizens were mildly curious but largely accepted the view it was nothing to do with them and, provided they could still go about their own business, they were unconcerned. Some of the more affluent merchants and artisans were more interested. They or their ancestors had been uprooted from their native country and any kind of change to the established order of things in the town was therefore a potential cause for concern.

Ridolphus called to see Sir Guy and Philippe one evening. "I have today received a communication from his holiness Pope Clement. I am sure it is only a coincidence he is resident in France under the protection of King Phillip, but he has issued a papal bull instructing all Christian monarchs to arrest all members of the Templar Order of Knights and seize their assets. I will, of course, pass this news on to all my brother monks – immediately we arrive in Strata Florida. We leave in the morning and I wish you both God's blessing in your endeavours." The pair thanked him and knelt before him in prayer. Then he departed and it was, as he had said, the last time they would ever see him.

Guy was managing to cope with the loss of his father and the departure of the monks from the town but now Philippe raised yet another concern. "I am sorry to bring yet another trouble to your door my friend" he apologised. "But we must consider again the safety of the relics in our care, especially the Ark itself." "I thought your engineers were making the hiding place under the church invulnerable to all but faithful Knights of the Order?" "This is true" replied Philippe. "Only those who have the secrets of our Order will know how to reach the sanctum we are preparing. But we are mere mortals and if many people attempt to reach it there is a chance that one day they may be successful. We must try to ensure the town remains a place of peace and that, long after we are both returned to dust, it never falls under the control of just one person – such as the vain or avaricious King of France."

Chapter 25

Simon, Vicki and Tim awoke on day three of their expedition to be greeted by another gloriously sunny spring morning. There was a little table outside the back of the cottage and although the weather wasn't too warm they decided to sit there for coffee and breakfast and to take in the simple beauty of their surroundings.

A grassy bank behind the cottage was covered in a mass of wild primroses and although the trees weren't quite in leaf yet they were bursting with life – as if waiting for some secret signal to all explode into leaf together. There was no roar of traffic either near or distant and no wind to rustle the trees, but the silence was broken by birdsong. Even the unfamiliar ear could pick out the sound of a Robin and Blackbird and the occasional squawk of a Jackdaw.

The whole Laugharne thing left a number of puzzling questions: why was the existence of the monastery covered up? Why did Guy de Bryan make over his lands to the townspeople of Laugharne by setting up the Corporation? And, if the treasure wasn't in the castle or the monastery, where else was it likely to be?

"Right guys, after breakfast we'll go back in and set up a whiteboard and have a proper brainstorm session" announced Simon. Vicki and Tim looked at each and giggled. "Yes teacher" said Tim, while Vicki sucked in her cheeks and fluttered her eyes in mock schoolgirl fashion. Simon grinned in return but justified his comment, saying "well I reckon if we're going to do this, we might as well treat it like a proper intelligence op. We put the ideas, comments and questions on the board and see what links, clues etc we have to tie them together."

With breakfast cleared away and the whiteboard set up they began their session. "Question one: Why was the existence of the monastery covered up?" began Simon. "Because they didn't want people to know it had existed" Tim trotted out the obvious answer without even thinking about it – he had been here so many times before. Simon was scribbling away on the board and then said "but why wouldn't you want people to know? Who would that be protecting and who would it be protecting them from?"

"If it was protecting the monks, it could be protecting them from the Knights Templar wanting their treasure back? Or from the Church? Or er, I dunno" suggested Vicki. "Ok, who else?" demanded Simon "who else might it be protecting?" "The people of the town?" "Ok – motive?" asked Simon. "Don't know." "Anyone else?" "The Templar Knights?" "Yes! Good one" agreed Simon. "Protecting them from who?" "Well, we know they're on the run from France...and the Knights left behind in France are being arrested all over the place and charged with heresy." "Yes...and?" encouraged Simon. "The record shows that not many years after Phillip had the Templars arrested he persuaded the Pope to outlaw them all together. So... if you were protecting the Templars, their next enemy after the king of France would have been the Church."

"And if there was a monastery in Laugharne, they would have been bound to know about the Templar Knights and would have been obliged to have turned them in" she added. "Do you think the monks could have taken the treasure from the Knights and then tried to cover their tracks?" asked Tim, looking at the scribbles on the board. "Hmmm" mused Simon. "Unlikely I would have thought. You've got a group of the best trained soldiers in Medieval Europe fired up to protect their treasure and taking shelter in an established defensive position. I wouldn't have thought they would easily have lost their treasure to a group of monks."

"Ok, so if it was to protect the Templars from discovery by the Church, do you think the monks took all the Templar treasure with them?" "I can't imagine that if your mission was to protect your treasure that you would simply hand it over to someone else the minute you arrived in Britain," said Simon. "So... was the grail the monks took with them a pay off?" "Yeah, I guess it could've been to buy their silence but it's unlikely we'll ever know" said Simon.

"Anyway, let's work on the theory that hiding or removing the existence of the monastery was to deliberately create some space between the monks and the Templars. If the monks then moved away to Strata Florida it's reasonable to suppose it was the Knights that stayed in or near Laugharne. And if they stayed in Laugharne, then they would have kept their treasure nearby. So, what's the next question?" Simon was beginning to get into his stride and beginning to enjoy the exercise.

"Well if we accept the Templars and their treasure remained in Laugharne, the other strange thing to happen at that time was Guy de Bryan making over his lands to the people of Laugharne in the form of Laugharne Corporation," observed Tim. "The Corporation was created in 1290 or 1307, depending on which source you look at. But if we assume it happened in the same year the Knights arrived with their treasure, why would he have done it?" asked Tim.

"If the grail was a payoff to the monks, then perhaps Guy de Bryan's lands were some kind of payoff to the local population?" suggested Vicki. "Yes, true – or could there have been something else? Like a tax dodge or a need to have spiritual forgiveness?" mused Simon.

"I doubt it," said Tim. "If the townspeople paid their rents to a Corporation instead of direct to Sir Guy then under Norman law the money would continue to flow into the Corporation – and back to the locals – even when Guy the elder died." "Ok, that might be a possibility – what about the spiritual side?" "I don't think it would have been that either" answered Tim. "If wealthy people wanted to protect their immortal soul they could simply buy their way into heaven by giving land or property to the Church."

"Right, so far then, we've decided the monastery was hidden to protect the location of the Templars. The Templars are likely to have stayed in Laugharne with the treasure and Guy de Bryan created Laugharne Corporation either as a massive payoff to the townspeople or as some kind of tax deal." "That's about it," agreed Tim.

By now it was approaching midday and as the sun was still shining they decided to walk to the Carpenter's Arms and celebrate their progress with a pint. "See? I knew a proper session would be productive" said Simon, only to be greeted by lots of forelock tugging and 'ooo aars' from his two companions. They couldn't quite make out his reply as he strode on ahead, but the second word definitely sounded like 'off.'

Chapter 26

After a couple of beers and some lunch at the pub, the mood amongst the little group was increasingly optimistic as they walked back to continue their research at the cottage. Simon's whiteboard exercise had, to their surprise, made progress. They now felt sure the monks had left Laugharne to protect the Templars and their treasure and they thought it likely the treasure was still hidden somewhere in or near the township.

It was most likely to have been hidden in a holy place of some sort and as close as possible to the castle. Back at the cottage they unfolded a local OS map of the area on the table and after a brief search decided there were four likely candidates: the nearest to the castle was the lost site of the monastery while a short distance to the west was the Norman church of Llansadurnen. To the north of the castle lay another ancient church at Llandawke but the closest place to the castle after the monastery was Laugharne church – the very first place they had seen when they first visited the area.

"How did we manage to forget Laugharne church?" said Simon. They had been so focussed on the castle and then the monastery that they had overlooked the impressive medieval structure that greeted all who entered Laugharne by road. Scrabbling for the reference books they discovered it was likely to have been a Roman temple that was rebuilt by Sir Guy de Bryan. "When did that happen?" Simon asked." Tim was rapidly skimming through the information: "it says here that it was probably by Sir Guy de Bryan in about 1350."

"That's interesting. Given the amount of time it took them to construct such substantial buildings they could well have started work on it just after the Templars arrived in 1307" mused Simon. "What else do we know about it" he asked. Tim continued reading. "The church is in a cruciform shape and lies almost due east to west. This is in keeping with most churches and is based on the belief that the second coming will appear from the direction of the rising sun in the east.

"Worshippers enter the nave of the church at the western end of the building and from here look up through the chancel to the sanctuary where the altar is placed. The 'arms' of the cross are found at the chancel and are known as the north transept and south transept."

"What about inside the church?" asked Simon. "Do we have any gems of information about that?" Tim looked down a list of 'things to note' selecting any items from the 14th Century or earlier. "There's a stoup in the south transept" he began. "A what?" After more searching they discovered a stoup was a recessed bowl containing holy water. In a custom inherited by the Catholic Church from the Jewish faith visitors would wash themselves before entering the church. "There's a stained glass window in the Nave depicting the de Bryan coat of arms and there are two 14th Century niches either side of the altar."

"Listen to this" Tim continued. "It says there is a low altar tomb in the sanctuary which is thought to be the tomb of Sir Guy de Bryan, senior." The three were warming to the idea that it might be the church, rather than either the castle or monastery, that held the Templar treasure. Simon summarized their discoveries: "the Templars arrive in 1307 seeking help from their old ally Sir Guy senior. We think the monks disappeared to Strata Florida to put space between them and the Templars, taking the grail with them as a gift or a payoff. Then Sir Guy senior dies and the record shows the church – which appears to have his tomb in it – was rebuilt around the same time.

"What better opportunity could you have to build a sacred hiding place than when rebuilding a church in memory of your Crusader comrade?"

Vicki had yet to visit the church and Simon and Tim's first visit had only been very brief. "Let's nip down there now and have a quick look around shall we?" suggested Simon. The other two agreed so they climbed into the car and headed off to St Martin's Church. They parked in the church car park where Simon and Tim had stopped during their first visit and walked up to the entrance to the church. The heavy door swung open and the trio were greeted by the aroma familiar in so many old churches of damp earth and candle smoke.

The place was deserted so they were free to examine the building without hindrance. They took in a vast painting in the nave, they studied the marble plaques on the walls and they moved up towards the chancel. They found the stoup in the south transept and a wooden chest containing the remains of a prehistoric burial discovered elsewhere in the town in the 1950s.

Passing up through the chancel they came to the step that signified the boundary of the sanctuary. This is where worshippers knelt in front of the altar to receive communion. Checking no-one was around, Simon stepped up into the sanctuary and moved around to the back of the altar. "What are you doing?" asked Vicki in a whisper. She wasn't a particularly religious person but she still had an innate respect for the sanctity of such places. "Look" answered Simon, as Tim crouched down beside him. "This is the tomb of our man. This is the tomb of Sir Guy de Bryan senior, the one the Templars came to for help."

He looked at Tim: "Wouldn't you like to see what's really buried under this tomb?" The pair grinned at each other. Vicki had remained in front of the altar and was feeling slightly uncomfortable: "we agreed that we would do things properly," she reminded them. "No digging things up or treasure hunting without the permission to do so and that way we can be open and honest about anything we find." They knew she was right but Simon was not to be put off. "It's OK Honey; I wasn't going to do anything – just having a look that's all."

"Everything we've looked at tells me this is the right place. I just want to have a look before we bother anyone with requests for permission." "How are you going to do that?" asked Vicki. "I've got an endoscope in the back of the van and if I pop it down through the gap in the top of the tomb here it will show us what's really inside." By now there was only a short amount of daylight left and there wouldn't be time to get back to the van and fetch the endoscope so they agreed to wait until the following morning.

Chapter 27

The following morning Vicki still had misgivings about Simon's idea to push a camera down into the altar of the church. She shared their optimism that they had indeed found the right place but she wanted to be sure they had consent before doing anything further. Consequently it was just Simon and Tim that set off to the church with the endoscope. Vicki would stay at the cottage and read her book.

The pair drove down towards the Grist en route to the church which lay at the opposite end of the town. As they reached the Grist they were surprised to see the estuary had risen up over the car park below the castle and the sea had spread right across the square. "Of course," said Simon "the spring and autumn tides are much higher than the rest of the year. Given how much the harbour has silted up over the years I'll bet the floods were quite significant when the monastery was here." "Hmm, you wouldn't want to be digging underground hiding places with all this water around would you?" mused Tim. They agreed it only made the case for the church look stronger.

Simon and Tim entered the church and stood looking at the tomb of Sir Guy de Bryan, the man whose coat of arms had led on a trail from France all the way to this far flung corner of Wales. Simon had brought the endoscope in a small carry case and he laid it on the floor next to the tomb, sprung the catches and opened it to reveal what looked like a mobile phone on a carry handle and attached to a long tube. "Let me introduce you to Wendy" he said "or, to give her full name, Bendy Wendy."

"What the Hell is it?" asked Tim. "Ah, this is what they call an endoscope or, more correctly, a military endoscope." Simon explained that unlike the endoscopes used in medicine, this one was designed to be fed under or around obstacles such as doors or through small holes in walls to see what was on the other side.

"Absolutely bloody marvellous things when we used them in the military, I can tell you. They helped us surprise a terrorist or two on more than one occasion." "Where did you get it?" asked Tim. "When I knew we were coming down here I thought it might be useful so I borrowed it from an old mate of mine. He kept it as a 'souvenir' from our past adventures. It's had a hard life so I hope it still works."

Simon removed it from the case, adding "I changed the batteries before we came" and fed the end of the probe into the top of the tomb through a small gap between the lid and the rear side. "Ok, let's see what we can see." The small screen gave a wide-angle image that showed all four inside walls of the tomb. Curiously, there was no coffin to be seen nor any decayed remains of a body or anything else, just empty space. "Hmm, looks like our man has gone walkabout" muttered Simon. He pushed the probe further into the tomb, but all it could pick up was a gaping hole where the base of the tomb should be and something else.

"Have a look at that" he said to Tim, offering him a closer look at the screen. "What do you make of that?" he asked. "It's difficult to make it out" answered Tim but I think... I think it looks like steps going down into the darkness?" "Yes, that's what I think too" agreed Simon. "Wow!" breathed Tim "do you think that's where the Templars hid the Ark of the Covenant?" "Well it's a funny place to put the entrance to a crypt" said Simon. "Besides I don't think this church has got a crypt anyway so, yes, I do think there's something of interest hidden down there."

"Come on" he said to Tim "give us a hand to prize this side off and have a look around." "Er, no" said Tim "I don't think we should." "What! Are you nuts?" Simon retorted. "We've spent all this time and effort chasing this bloody treasure and now you're backing out?" "No, no – it's not that," answered Tim. "Well what then?"

"Well you remember when we were in the tunnel under the castle? We weren't supposed to be there and because of that we weren't able to make any record of what we'd found. If this really is the greatest discovery of the Century, I want to be sure we can make a proper record of it and tell people about it. Besides, Vicki isn't here and you promised her not to do anything other than look."

"Alright, I understand you want to do it properly, but all we would be doing is having a little look around first? Just to make sure? pleaded Simon. Tim paused, then said: "look, we're in a church on our own and you want to go down into some kind of underground hiding place without any equipment, without any official permission and without any backup. This could be 1000 years old and if it is, we have no idea of the condition it's in. Nor do we know if there are any booby traps to catch out the unwary. If we got into trouble or needed help, think what people would say if we had to be rescued – think what it would do to Vicki."

They were both surprised at Tim's maturity and Simon, despite being more excited about the hunt than he had ever been, felt he had to concede to the wisdom of his younger friend. After all, his experience and training had shown what could happen when launching an op without prior planning. They withdrew the endoscope and packed it back into its case and draped the back of the altar cloth into its rightful position.

"Ok, so what do we do next?" asked Simon, as they stood looking at the altar. "I'm not sure" answered Tim "but we need to get permission to open the place up properly. I don't know who we ask but I'm sure they're going to need a bit of convincing to let us do what we want to do." "Ok, we'll tell Vicki we've seen steps going down into presumably some kind of secret underground chamber," said Simon. "Then we'll need to find out the proper procedure to make this treasure hunt legal."

As they walked down the aisle towards the door a text message pinged onto Simon's phone. He unlocked the phone and saw the text was from Vicki. When he read it his knees buckled and he nearly dropped to the floor in shock "Jesus Christ!" he said. "What? What the fuck's the matter? asked Tim. Without saying a word, Simon just handed him the phone. Tim looked at it and his blood ran cold. The message said 'I HAVE YOUR WIFE. NO POLICE AND SHE WON'T GET HURT. WAIT FOR MY INSTRUCTIONS.' There was also a photo of Vicki, her hair completely dishevelled, her face red and tear stained and a scarf tied across her mouth as a gag.

Simon had now recovered and he was filled instead with an uncontrollable, raging anger. "I'm going to find the bastard that's done this and I'm going to fucking kill him" he shouted as he ran towards the door and his car. "Come on! Move! Move! Move!" he shouted over his shoulder at Tim.

Chapter 28

The question of how to protect the township from ever falling under the control of someone tempted to plunder its secrets challenged Guy and Philippe late into the night without any answer coming forth. The following day, Guy was engaged in the work of administering the township's rules and affairs. It had perforce been neglected somewhat of late and there was much to catch up on. One of the last tasks of the day was to meet one of the cockle gatherers who lived in a hovel on the seashore. The man was perhaps 22 or 23 years of age, just over 5 foot tall and typical of the stocky, slightly swarthy appearance of the Celtic race.

He clenched and unclenched his knitted woollen cap nervously in his strong, calloused hands and spoke in Welsh through an interpreter. "May it please your Lordship but may I have permission to cut reeds from the beds on the Marsh to repair our home? The roof has fallen in: we have no shelter from the rain and my mother lies sick in her cot." Guy realised the man dare not take the reed without permission and he felt sorry that he, Guy, had been too busy to deal with the matter sooner. He gave consent without hesitation and also instructed that Brother Jerome, whom Ridolphus had instructed to stay behind to tend to the sick, should visit the man's mother.

The cockle gatherer fell to his knees in thanks at the gesture and spoke rapidly to the interpreter before backing out of the room, bowing as he went. "He is grateful to your Lordship," explained the interpreter "and is fetching a sack of cockles in thanks." Those cockles would be the greatest thing of value the man possessed, mused Guy and he fell to thinking how a good Christian might assist others in a similar situation.

Then he remembered something of which his father had often spoken when discussing his fondness for the people of the town. Gradually the idea took on a clearer form. If he could gain Royal approval, his father's plan with some minor changes offered, he believed, a solution that would keep the town out of the clutches of any dishonourable nobility in the future and benefit even the lowliest of its inhabitants into the bargain. He spoke to Philippe about the idea. "It is certainly very generous to the people of Talacharn" agreed Philippe. He could also see how it would stop the township being bargained for or fought over by successive generations with ambitions for any hidden treasures rumoured to exist.

"Very well," said Guy at last. "This will require the consent of King Edward. I shall ask for it to be granted in the name of my late father." He called for his clerk and, together with Philippe, they arranged for the deed to be drawn up and presented to the King for Royal assent.

The days passed until Christmas day itself arrived. As the Saxon church was still being rebuilt, Guy's chaplain Meurig held services of praise and thanksgiving at the old cross on the square. Fortunately although there had been snow on Christmas Eve, this day the sun shone and the festive atmosphere was throughout the town. Later that day the news arrived that Guy had been waiting for: the document from the King himself.

Guy wasted no time and sent out messengers to instruct everyone from the town that they should, by his command, gather again at the cross the following morning. It was a puzzled and curious crowd that assembled the next morning, stamping their feet against the cold and murmuring about what news could be so important.

Guy climbed onto the plinth below the cross. "I have this St Stephen's Day received assent from his gracious majesty King Edward to make a gift to the people of Talacharn as follows: to all the faithful in Christ, to whom this present writing shall come, I, Guy de Bryan wish you all eternal salvation in the Lord. Let all of you know that we have this day granted to our beloved and faithful burgesses of Talacharn for us and for our heirs and successors, whoever they may be, all the good laws and customs that the burgesses of Caerfyrddin have up to now used and enjoyed in the time of King John.

"We have also granted to the same men, a free common in all our northern wood and all that common pasture in the Marsh and also all that free common from the rivulet which is named Mackerel Lake, proceeding upwards as far as Greensladehead and towards the east over Eynons Down." Guy continued to read the Charter that he had gifted to Laugharne in the name of his father. The assembled crowd were amazed. Much of the land belonging to the lordship was now vested in a new body called the Corporation. Every man born in the township would, on reaching the age of 21, become a part of that Corporation. The members of the Corporation would choose their own officers to run the Corporation and choose a Portreeve to lead the Corporation.

"You are now free men. By order of the King, no-one can come to Talacharn and exercise dominion over the land and rights I have given to you in the name of my father." When he had finished speaking, a spontaneous cheer greeted him. Guy was cheered and applauded all the way back to the castle. The Charter, bearing the seal of the King, was posted on the door of the castle so that all could see it and those with learning could read it.

"I congratulate you my Lord Guy" said Philippe. "Your generosity has stemmed the rumours about the monastery and the church; has done much to assure the safety of the church – and its contents – and won the gratitude of the people of the town." "Thank you," said Guy. "Do not think the running of the township can now be put to one side. There will be much to do to help and advise the burgesses on how to establish and run their Corporation – and I will be looking to you and the Knights to help in these matters."

Philippe looked at Guy and grinned. "Today you may have become a poorer man in your worldly wealth. But you have become richer in so many other ways. You have done a wonderful thing and I offer my salue to you."

Chapter 29

Simon was sprinting towards the BMW and it was all Tim could do to get to the car before they launched out of the church car park in a hail of dust and gravel. "Simon for Christ's sake slow down!" he yelled as the car screamed through Laugharne's streets crowded with parked cars. They narrowly missed a lorry coming the other way and almost swiped the walls of some houses on the downhill towards the Grist square.

As they rose up the hill out of Laugharne, Simon had, very slightly, eased the pace although it was still too fast to be safe. "Where are we going?" Tim shouted. "Cottage first" came the reply through clenched teeth. The BMW roared up the little driveway to the cottage and slid to a halt in another cloud of dust and gravel.

Going in to the cottage, they could see it had been witness to a fierce struggle. There was an overturned lamp in the sitting room but the main destruction was in the kitchen. The table had been pushed to one side scattering mugs and papers everywhere and causing a potted plant to smash into pieces, shedding soil across the floor. A kitchen chair lay in splinters on its side and more worryingly there was a patch of blood and several large droplets on the floor and the side of the kitchen worktop. "Well at least she put up a fight" muttered Simon. "Good girl" he added.

Then he was heading back out to the car again with Tim running along behind. "Where are we going now?" he asked. "We're going to find the bastard that did this" answered Simon. They roared off down the driveway this time at a more controlled but still unnervingly fast pace. Within minutes they had arrived at the farmhouse belonging to Carwyn and Lucy Evans.

Simon was out of the car and pounding on the front door with his fist. "Where is he?" he shouted. Lucy Evans opened the door and Simon pushed past her into the entrance hall. "Where are you? Come out you bastard" he shouted as he stormed from room to room. Finding no-one, he returned to the front hallway where Lucy Evans was standing with Tim. "Where is he?" Simon demanded angrily. Lucy's eyes were wide with fear "he's out," she said "he had to go to London."

By now the small voice of conscience in the back of Simon's head was starting to make itself heard. He was still angry but he could see the terror in the woman's eyes and he felt a twinge of guilt at being the cause of it. "Tell him I want a word with him as soon as he gets home" he growled and walked back to his car. Tim gave the woman a look of apology and followed his friend to the car.

They drove away from the farm, this time at a legal speed. "What the fuck was all that about?" demanded Tim. It was his turn to feel hurt and angry. "You nearly fucking kill us driving like a maniac and then you barge into that woman's home and scare the living daylights out of her!" "Think about it" Simon replied, clenching and unclenching his hands on the steering wheel as he did so. "Who else knows about what we're doing here? Who else knows what the stakes are and who else knows where we're staying?" Tim had to concede it was only Carwyn Evans that ticked all the boxes.

"But what is he thinking?" asked Tim. "Surely he must know he can't get away with pulling a stunt like this – if that's what he's doing?" "That's the point, he's not thinking" answered Simon. "Some strangers rock up at his wife's cottage and it turns out they're searching for something that even on the black market would be worth more money than you could spend in a lifetime. He's an ex-copper with a chip on his shoulder because the bad guys are always the ones to get away with it and he thinks to himself, this is my big chance. A bit of fast work and I get to live on my own tropical island – probably alongside all those bastards he's spent years trying to catch."

"Well what do we do now?" asked Tim. "I don't know," answered Simon. "I don't know where he is, I don't know where Vicki is. All we can do is wait at the cottage until we hear from him again." They returned to the cottage and began to tidy up the damage as best they could. "Should we phone the police?" Tim asked. Simon thought about it then said "If he's an ex-copper he'll probably know all the tricks they use in situations like this – and I don't want to risk Vicki getting hurt. My feeling is we just sit tight until he gets in touch."

They had just about finished getting the place straight when a police car came crunching gently up the gravel drive and two uniformed police officers, a man and a woman, got out of the car and knocked at the door. "Good morning officers, how can I help you?" asked Simon. "Can we come in sir?" said the man, very politely. "We've had a report of an incident at a farm near here in which you were involved. The lady seemed quite upset and said you had pushed your way into her house, demanding to see her husband?" "Er, yes that's true, I'm afraid. I had a business agreement with him and I thought he was not going to stick to the agreement, causing me considerable hardship. I was angry and did not mean to upset his wife." The two officers looked at him and for a moment said nothing. Then the man said "Well there was no damage and the lady said you didn't touch her or threaten her directly and she didn't want to press charges." "Oh right, thank you officer" said Simon.

The police officers stood up to leave and as they passed out of the door the man turned and said "we also heard earlier of a car of a similar description to yours being driven dangerously through Laugharne." Then he paused, before adding: "If you want my advice, start behaving yourself like a normal businessman or you'll be spending time in the cells while I put together a list of criminal charges." Simon just looked at him as he walked out through the door. "Shit, that was lucky" he said as they disappeared down the drive. "Now all we can do is wait."

Chapter 30

1307 had become a year for the ordinary people of Talacharn to give great thanks. Under Norman law they were now free men. Free of the yoke of feudal dues and able to graze their livestock and feed their families under the simple governance of their peers.

For Guy it was a busy time, helping the burgesses form their first jury, and choosing the officers of the court including the foreman, recorder, common attorneys, halberdiers and their own Portreeve. The inauguration of the first Portreeve, the first leader of the Corporation chosen from amongst its own, was an occasion for much celebration and feasting and services of thanksgiving by Sir Guy's – and now the Portreeve's – chaplain.

Later in the year was held the Common Walk. Books, maps and writing were still the preserve of the few. For the majority, the observation of rules and boundaries was learned and passed on through oral means. Knowing the boundaries of Corporation land was essential to avoid disputes with other landowners so the townspeople gathered and walked the boundaries of their Corporation together. Every corner, thicket and crossing place had its own name and these were given out to the assembled crowd. Woe betide any who would forget the name of the place.

Meanwhile the Templars continued their construction of the new church dedicated to the memory of Sir Guy de Bryan and of his generosity to the town. A Templar sergeant, who had been with Philippe at Acre in the Holy Land, explained the works to him. "The church will be much larger than the old Saxon church and we are adding a new chancel and sanctuary to the east of the old church. We shall build a tower with turret and a transept to form the shape of the cross," he added.

"What about the sanctuary for the Ark?" asked Philippe. "How goes the work for that?" "We are digging down through the sandstone but we have found a spring that looks like it was a shrine of some sort used by the Romans." "Will this cause much difficulty?" asked Philippe. "Not at all" replied the sergeant "we had planned to use a wooden door to protect the sanctum but we think if we can use the weight of the water to help raise it, then we can craft a door made of stone in its stead." "Very good, it is well" nodded Philippe.

Time passed and although the building of the new church was helped by using dressed limestone and other materials from the old monastery it was still many summers before the work was completed. Eventually the sergeant was able to say "it is finished." The people of the township were invited to gaze upon the majesty and splendour that was their new church.

The first thing they noticed was just how big it was. After the castle it was the second largest building in the township. Its tower with corner turret equalled the height of the castle. Inside, the friends of Sir Guy's father had created a magnificent space with glorious ceilings and intricate carvings. Rising up from the nave of the church through the chancel lay the sanctuary and in it was the tomb of Sir Guy the elder carved in intricate ogee-patterned stone.

With their work completed, the small band of Templars gradually faded away from the life of the township. Some set aside their vow of chastity and settled into a quiet life of retirement with a local girl. Others sought passage back to their native France as ordinary citizens while some joined the monastery in Whitland. Philippe himself had become an old man and finished his days in Talacharn castle as an honoured companion of Sir Guy.

As for Sir Guy, he had been a young man when the Templars first arrived. He met and married Gwenllian, daughter of Gryfydd ap Lloyd, and in due course she bore him a son. This Guy de Bryan rose to become the Lord High Admiral of Edward III, was made one of the first Knights of the Garter when the order was instituted in 1348 and was honoured to have the Bryan coat of arms emblazoned on the chest that held the Treaty of Calais during the Hundred Years War.

Although the Templar Order was now disbanded, the dwindling group of men that had made the dangerous voyage across the sea in the autumn of 1307 continued to worship at the Ark of the Covenant at least twice a year at Christmas and Easter. They would enter the church in the dead of night when no-one was around and ease back the stone of Sir Guy's tomb. Then they would roll onto the steps that led down to the sanctum, sealed and protected from all but the faithful of the Templar Order.

Over the years the occasional light had been seen from their lamps but whenever anyone entered the church there was nothing and no-one to be seen. The reports of mysterious lights gave birth to numerous stories of ghosts or other strange happenings. That only served to strengthen the protection given to the Ark and keep away the curious.

Chapter 31

After receiving the text message and the furious events that followed, the rest of that Thursday was an agony of waiting for Simon and Tim. They had no idea where Vicki was being kept prisoner and they had decided it was too risky to involve the police. "Should we call Vicki's parents?" asked Tim. "Yeah, I thought about that" said Simon. "But what could they do to help? All it would do is get them worried. They might even want to come down here and I can't look after them if we're dealing with this."

The waiting was eating into their psyche, wearing them down. But Simon knew he had to fight it – he had to stay strong. When the moment came he needed to be ready to act; ready to rescue his Vicki. His mobile phone pinged with another text message. He grabbed it and, fighting the tremble in his hands, read the message:

"Why were police there?"
"Driving incident. Told them nothing"
"Be at church tonight at 9.00. You and your friend. Bring van with full tank fuel"
"Is Vicki OK?"
"Be there at 9.00 and all OK. Otherwise be sorry."

Simon showed the texts to Tim. "So, we were right" said Tim. "He's after the treasure and needs us to help shift it." The treasure no longer held any appeal for Simon. All he wanted was to get his beloved Vicki back. In past years when he had faced difficult times as a soldier and then later when he was lost on rejoining civilian life, she had stood by him. She had soothed him during the nightmares; she had given him hope and encouragement when he could see none. She was his rock. The foundation on which his whole world stood. He would give his last breath to see her safe – and meet a terrible retribution on those who had dared harm her.

The van had just over half a tank of fuel so they drove to St Clears to top it up and then returned to the cottage to wait once more. Tim sprawled in an armchair and tried to sleep. Simon started reading a novel he found in the cottage. Neither were successful in their activities as all they could do was wait. The clock said half past and they would wait an age before looking at it again – it said ten minutes had passed.

Eventually however, the sun sank below the horizon and nightime descended. Although it was now late spring and the days were getting longer, the sun still set by 8.30 and it was well and truly dark by 9.00, especially if the weather was overcast as it was tonight. They drove the van through Laugharne to the church car park, drew up next to the steps and went inside the church to wait.

It was another 30 minutes before their antagonist appeared before them. "Good evening gentlemen" said the figure. "What the fuck are you doing here?" it was Tim who was most shocked. They had expected to see Carwyn Evans but the man in front of them was Tim's boss from the bookshop in Oxford, John Impey. "You seem surprised" said Impey. "You could fucking say that again" said Tim. Simon was shocked but he looked straight at Impey and growled "where's my wife you bastard?" He went to lunge at the man but Impey raised his arm from his side and waved him back: "Steady on Major, there's no need for things to get ugly" he cautioned and Simon and Tim saw Impey was holding a gun, a Colt .45 automatic pistol.

"Now, we've got a lot to do tonight, so the sooner we get on with it the sooner it will all be over and the sooner you will get your wife back" said Impey. As his eyes adjusted to the torchlight, Simon could see Impey bore several deep scratch marks down the side of his face, one remarkably close to his eye. "Did my wife give you those?" he asked. "She was remarkably uncooperative I have to say," came the reply. Good, thought Simon as they made their way to the altar and the tomb of Guy de Bryan.

"I don't get it" Tim was saying. "What on earth are you doing John? Why are you throwing away all you've done with the bookshop to do this?" "Oh Tim, don't be so naive my dear boy," said Impey. "Back in the day I was making big money – I mean really big money – importing herbal products from Morocco. I had the smart suits, the designer watches, expensive cars and more sexy birds than you could shake a stick at. It was fun!

"But now look at me; for years I've been running a dry as dust old bookshop in Oxford, waiting to come across that priceless manuscript; that rare first edition: being nice to College professors who are soo fucking boring. And look at me, I wear supermarket clothes and drive a crappy old Citroen. This is my last chance to get back to where I was. With this treasure I can retire and live like a king!"

"This is crazy!" said Tim. "You don't need to do this! – we're going to get permission to get this treasure legally – and you can come in with us." His pleading fell on deaf ears. "Huh! You think by the time you've got permission and the church has given you a share of their share, then you've given me a share of your share that it's going to be worth anything? I don't think so! Now if you don't mind, we've got work to do."

They reached the tomb and Impey ordered them to remove the altar cloth and crucifix and place them to one side. "OK, smash it open" he ordered and Tim was about to bring a sledgehammer down on the stone slab when Simon stopped him. "You don't need to do that" he said. "Look, it was designed so the rear panel folds out and you just roll onto the staircase." He lifted the rear panel and, sure enough, it pivoted out to leave a space big enough for a man to climb in, lying on his side.

"We haven't got time for that. Smash the top open," said Impey. Reluctantly, the two men did as they were told. When they had finished and removed the debris, it revealed a flight of about thirty steps leading down to a heavy oak door. "On you go," ordered Impey and down the steps they went, with Impey following at a safe distance behind. Despite its great age, the door was solid as a rock. Thick metal straps set into the stone on one side provided the hinges and on the other side was a large keyhole protected by a metal escutcheon.

There was a Latin inscription carved into the wood. "Translate that for me Tim" ordered Impey. Tim raised his torch and studied the words. "It's a warning. It says no stranger is to enter within the temple and enclosure. Whoever is caught will be himself responsible for his ensuing death. Do you still want to go on?" The warning was dismissed by Impey: "load of mumbo jumbo" he said. "Break it down."

They tried some blows with sledgehammers but they just bounced off the door with no effect. "Looks like it's over Impey" said Simon. "We could be here all night but you're not going to get this door open without power tools." Impey was quiet for a moment but then he said "You think so? Reach up and grab that object on the ledge just above the door." From his vantage point a little higher up the stairs Impey's powerful electric torch had been able to pick out an object that would have been invisible in the weaker light of a medieval lamp or candle.

Simon reached above his head and ran his fingers along the stone ledge. They struck a metal object that he grasped and brought down where they could see it. Unbelievably, it was a large metal key. "Is this when the traditional hiding place for door keys was invented?" he said to Tim. The humour was lost in the situation, but Simon pushed the key into the lock. He and Tim looked at each other as the key slotted into place. "Come on, come on! Open it!" ordered the voice above them.

The key turned in the lock and with the two of them pulling and tugging on the loop handle, the door slowly swung open.

Chapter 32

The heavy door swung open to reveal yet more steps downwards. These lead to a room that was rectangular in shape, about 20 feet across and 40 feet long. There was what looked like a small altar at the far end, opposite the doorway. An enormous wall hanging decorated each of the side walls, with the third wall hanging, the largest one, on the wall behind the altar. It looked as if the material had at one time been richly coloured and decorated but the years of accumulated dirt and mould meant now they were just a blotchy crimson colour. In the centre of the room was a stone tomb, facing the altar and bare, save for a magnificent gold and jewel-decorated sword on its lid.

Impey gave a short, slightly hysterical laugh of disbelief. "Is this it? Is this the famous treasure you were going to find for me? Where's the fucking treasure you morons!" he screamed. Simon was almost relieved "what are you going to do now?" he said, looking straight at Impey. "Give me that sword" came the reply. "Carefully! If you want to see your wife again."

Simon picked the sword from the tomb and stepped across the room to the bottom of the staircase and handed it to the man by its hilt. Carefully Impey retreated backwards up the stairs keeping his gun pointed at them at all times. At the doorway he threw the sword behind him and with his free hand reached for the door and slammed it shut, twisting the key in the lock before Simon and Tim could get to him. His voice muffled by the great door, they heard him say "Don't worry I'm sure someone will let you out in the morning when they find the mess you've made up here. I'll be far enough away by then and I'll let you have my ransom demand."

With that he was gone.

They stepped back into the room, powerless to do anything but wait. After pacing up and down, they sat on the cold stone floor, Simon leaning against Guy de Bryan's tomb and Tim next to the altar. To their surprise they heard a noise up above followed by the sound of the key turning in the lock. The door once again swung slowly open and a voice said "We've really got to stop meeting like this boys." It was Carwyn Evans. Simon was delighted and embarrassed at the same time: "Look, er, I owe you an apology I'm afraid" he began. "There's no need, I understand the situation" said Carwyn. "I'd be pretty angry if someone threatened my Lucy, so you're lucky you didn't go that far."

"How did you know? I mean how did you find us?" asked Tim. "After your visit, Lucy phoned me and sounded pretty upset. I got on a train and came straight back from London. When I got back to Laugharne I went straight round to the cottage. I saw the broken chair and some smears of blood on the floor and guessed something bad had happened. Then I remembered seeing your van parked in the church car park and when I came over to investigate I saw lights moving in the church. I guessed what you might be up to and crept into the church to find out.

"When I saw your friend out there was carrying a gun I caught him by surprise and disarmed the bugger." "Where is he now?" asked Simon. "Waiting out there, I guessed you might want to have a chat with him" Carwyn grinned. The three climbed out of the crypt and made their way down the church to the entrance where Impey sat in a pew, bound hand and foot with cable ties. Simon was pleased to note the scratches on his face had now been joined by a swollen lip that dribbled blood onto his chin and shirt.

"Right you bastard, where's my wife?" he said, grabbing Impey by the collar. He had wanted to beat the man to a pulp but now all he wanted was to get Vicki back safely. Impey hesitated, so Simon reached down with his other hand and grabbed the man's testicles, squeezing them hard. "Alright, alright!" yelped Impey. "She's on a boat I've chartered, the Blue Endeavour. It's moored at Neyland" he said.

"So what were you going to do?" asked Simon. "Take the treasure and drown her?" Impey explained his plan had been to get Simon and Tim to load the treasure onto the boat from the van. Then he was going to sail on the morning tide for Europe, releasing the three of them in a dinghy when they were safely out at sea. "By the time you had got back to land and raised the alarm I could have been long gone" he said. "I wouldn't have hurt you or her, that's not my thing" he added.

Carwyn agreed to stay with Impey in the church and phone for the police while Simon and Tim went in search of Vicki. Simon shook him by the hand "Thank you" he said. "And I'm sorry for what I did." Carwyn smiled: "Go on, go and find your wife" he said. Simon and Tim drove the van back to the cottage and transferred to the BMW. It would be faster and the sat nav could show them exactly where they needed to go.

Despite Simon's vigorous driving, the journey still took about three-quarters of an hour. The marina lay on the Cleddau river and was faced by a smart row of modern houses that looked like they had been built for yachting enthusiasts. "Shit there's bloody loads of boats here. Where do we start?" said Tim. There was nothing for it but to start at one end and work their way along every jetty. Simon was on the sixth jetty when Tim shouted from the next one along "Simon. Over here!"

Simon sprinted along the timber jetties to where Tim was waiting. There lay the Blue Endeavour, a neat 34 foot yacht, fully equipped and ready to sail. They climbed on board and slid back the hatch to the cabin. Tim found a switch and turned on the cabin lights. Simon gently pushed open the door to one of the forward bunks and as it swung open the light shone on Vicki, lying on the bed, tied hand and foot and gagged with the scarf he had seen in the photo message. He lunged forward and pulling the scarf from her face he held her to him. "Oh my Darling, my Darling" he whispered clutching her tightly and rocking back and forth as the tears streamed down his face. Vicki looked at him and burst into tears, her whole body rocking with every sob.

Tim had found a small knife in the galley and passed it to Simon to cut Vicki's bonds. They climbed out of the bunk into the main cabin and Vicki rubbed her wrists that were red and bruised. She looked at her husband, paused and said "I'm sorry, I wet myself, I couldn't help it" and with that came more huge convulsions of sobbing and tears. "It doesn't matter, it doesn't matter, I don't care, I love you my Darling" said Simon as he hugged and kissed her again and again.

As the tears gradually eased and they gained their composure, they felt able to leave the boat and make their way back to the car. "We'll stay at the cottage tonight and then go home in the morning," said Simon. He gave the car keys to Tim to drive and climbed into the back next to Vicki, where he could put his arm around her and comfort her for the journey.

Chapter 33

It was a little after 9.00 the following morning when there was a knock on the door of the cottage. Simon opened the door to a uniformed woman police officer and an officer in plain clothes who identified himself as Detective Sergeant Jenkins. They had come to take statements from all three "If you're ready to do so, sir" said DS Jenkins.

They went, one at a time, into the sitting room and gave their statements to the police. With the paperwork out of the way, Simon wanted to know if they were now allowed to return to Oxfordshire. The policeman confirmed they had all they needed for the time being and as they had provided all their contact details they could indeed go back to Oxfordshire whenever they wished. "What's happened to Mr Impey?" asked Tim. "We had a statement at the scene from Mr Evans so Mr Impey was kept in the cells overnight. Now we've got your statements we'll charge him later this morning," said DS Jenkins.

"I used to work for him" said Tim. "Do you have any idea what might happen to his bookshop now?" The policeman thought about it and said "Usually the family take over the running of a business when someone is arrested. If he has family that's what's likely to happen. Whether you want to continue working there is a matter for you sir." Tim didn't know yet what he was going to do.

After a shower, a good night's sleep and some breakfast Vicki had recovered something of her old self, but she was keen to get home as soon as possible. They decided Tim would drive the van back alone so Vicki could travel with Simon in the car. Simon and Vicki would go over to the Evans' on the way to apologize and to hand back the keys. They waved Tim off and then headed over to the Evans' farm.

Simon's knock at the front door was far more restrained and polite than it had been on the previous occasion. Lucy Evans opened the door and Simon's first words were those of apology "Mrs Evans, I'm so very sorry for my appalling behaviour yesterday morning" he began, but she cut him off: "Don't worry about it Major Kershaw. Carwyn told me the full story last night when he got home from the police station. If he'd been in your situation I know he would have been the same – or worse, probably," she added.

"You're very kind" said Simon. "I'm afraid there was some damage to the cottage, but if you let me know how much it comes to I'll pay the bill." Carwyn appeared in the hallway "Hello Simon. How is your wife?" "She's fine thanks. She's just out in the car. We're heading back to Oxfordshire." Simon declined the Evans' offer to them both to come in for a cup of tea or coffee but he did have a brief chat with Carwyn about the evening's events. Carwyn explained the police had turned up to take Impey away and he had gone with them to make a statement just to get it out of the way.

"What happened to the sword?" asked Simon. "Well that was a funny thing" said Carwyn. "I phoned the vicar to let him know what had happened and he got there well before the police. He just took the sword and as far as I could make out went down those steps at the altar, put it back in the crypt, locked the door and took the key home with him. He was upset that the top slab of the altar had been smashed but he didn't say anything at all about the secret steps or crypt." "Hmm. Strange indeed" agreed Simon. "Anyway, I've got to be going." With that Simon settled their accounts, repeated his apologies and they said their goodbyes.

The journey back to Witney was uneventful, Simon following Tim along the motorway to make the journey as quick as possible. Vicki's parents had not expected them back until the Saturday so were surprised when they arrived. It was decided to close the shop for the afternoon and they all adjourned to the flat to tell their story over a glass of wine. Vicki's parents were astonished at the behaviour of a man running such a respectable, solid business in Oxford and they were appalled at what had happened to their daughter. "What's happened to him now?" asked James Dolan. "He's been charged with criminal damage and kidnapping" said Simon. "We'll have to go back for the trial but they reckon he'll get a substantial jail sentence." "He's lucky the police got to him first" said James Dolan, without emotion. Simon looked at his retired spook of a father-in-law and thought to himself, yes he's probably right.

The Dolans thought it best to let their children have their flat to themselves tonight, so they packed their clothes and said their farewells around 6.00pm. Tim was ready to make his excuses and head back to his caravan but Simon and Vicki wouldn't hear of it. "I'll change the sheets and you can stay in the spare room" said Vicki. "Besides, you've had a few drinks so you can't drive home to... where are you now?" "Long Hanborough" "Well, you can't drive back to Long Hanborough tonight" Simon assured him.

They settled back for some more of Simon's red wine while Vicki, marvel that she was, not only made the spare room ready but also produced another amazing evening meal. As they sat around after dinner, enjoying cheese and biscuits with some vintage port, Tim said to Simon "Did you notice anything familiar about that crypt when we were shut in there?" "Not really, it's not the sort of place I tend to frequent" grinned Simon as he hugged Vicki to him on the sofa. Then he added "why, what are you getting at?"

"Have a look at this," said Tim and he flicked through one of the books they had brought back from Wales. He opened a thick hardback tome at an artist's impression of the Temple of Solomon. "I was thinking about this as I was driving back" he explained. "I think the room we were in looked a lot like the Holy Place in this drawing. It had an altar at the far end opposite the door just like this" he said, holding the picture up for Simon and Vicki to see. "Right...and?" said Simon. "Well" continued Tim "If that was a copy of the Holy Place, then the wall hanging behind the altar could represent the veil? The veil that hides the Holy of Holies?"

"Wow!" exclaimed Simon, sitting bolt upright and nearly spilling his drink. "What? I don't understand?" questioned Vicki. "The Temple of Solomon was on the Temple Mount in Jerusalem but was destroyed in about 600BC," explained Simon. "Then the site became the headquarters of the Knights Templar in Jerusalem and they spent many years tunnelling under it in search of the treasures from the original Temple. Rumour has it that amongst the treasure and relics they discovered was the Ark of the Covenant. The box in which Moses placed the Ten Commandments God had given to him in tablets of stone. It is said to have miraculous powers and be the means for communicating directly with God. The Ark was kept behind the veil in the Holy of Holies."

"But surely that was a solid wall behind that wall hanging?" said Simon. "That's what confused me," said Tim. "I think anyone entering that room and just looking at it would make a logical assumption that it was all solid. But when I sat on the floor and leaned against the material it went back much further than it should have done if it was against a solid wall – and in all the excitement I'd forgotten about it until I was driving back in the van." "You mean?" "Yes, everyone gets to that room and stops looking! All we've got to do is get behind that wall hanging!"

"Oooh No!" said Vicki, leaning away from them both. "We're not going back there again. Absolutely not. No!"

Chapter 34

Vicki was adamant she had already seen enough of Laugharne and wanted nothing more to do with Templar treasure, religious relics or any of it. "Look at all the trouble it has caused" she said. Simon tried to reason with her: "All we're saying is let's have a look behind the curtain. There's no danger in that surely?" Vicki was suddenly angry with the pair "You promised! You promised not to do anything else without having the proper permission."

Simon may have been excited but recent events demonstrated just how important Vicki was to him and he had no desire to go against her wishes. "OK, well if we get permission in writing from the appropriate source, can we just have a look then?" he asked. For her part Vicki did not want to stop her husband and his friend's search for the treasure even though she had been badly frightened by her recent experience so she grudgingly agreed.

It was Vicki's father that explained to them that getting permission to do anything in an Anglican church required the grant of something called a faculty from the Bishop in whose diocese the relevant property was located. Declining James Dolan's offer of help, Simon, with Vicki's assistance, drafted a letter to the Bishop of St Davids. They decided to mention the unfortunate events that ended in a forthcoming court case and stressed their investigation of the crypt in which they had been held captive would take only a matter of moments. No equipment would be used except for hand-held torches or lamps.

Simon posted the letter first-class. He was slightly surprised to receive a reply just a couple of days later, almost by return post. He showed the letter to Vicki and phoned Tim to share its contents: "It's quite mysterious" he said. "They say that in normal circumstances they would have declined the request but as we have been instrumental in minimising damage to the church and we prevented loss of a valuable artefact, it has been decided to grant our request. It goes on to specify that you, me, Vicki and Carwyn Evans are therefore invited to come to the church at 11.00am on the 4th of next month for a meeting with Church representatives."

"Sounds brilliant" said Tim. "I'm in." Simon called Carwyn to let him know about the letter, but he didn't mention what he and Tim believed was behind the wall hanging. The Evans' cottage wasn't available on the due date so Simon, Vicki and Tim booked into a nearby country house hotel and travelled down on the evening before the meeting. Carwyn and Lucy joined them for dinner that evening and there was an atmosphere of anticipation for what the morrow would bring together with some considerable leg pulling of Simon's previous behaviour.

Next morning the sun shone down from a clear blue sky. Every inch of grass seemed covered with either primroses or daffodils and the trees were now in open competition to put on as much fresh green leaf as possible. The country house where they were staying afforded a view out over Carmarthen Bay and Tim couldn't help but think of all the ships that over the centuries had sailed there, the cargoes they had carried and the people that had sailed in them.

They dressed for their meeting with the Church representatives. Not quite business suit, but still much smarter than had been the case during their previous visits. Carwyn met them in the car park and together they walked up to the church door. They were met at the door by two men in dark suits. "Good morning" said one. "Which one of you is Major Kershaw?" Simon reached out and shook the two men by the hand. "This is my wife Vicki," he said. "This is Tim Woodruff and Carwyn Evans"

The man who had spoken first said "Good morning all. My name is Taylor and this is my colleague Mr McLean. Before we go in, could I ask you all to sign this paper please? It's just a disclaimer against injury and a confidentiality agreement. It's just a formality that's all."

Simon felt uncomfortable about signing any such paper, but he couldn't think why. They all signed as requested and Taylor smiled, neatly folding each sheet before tucking them into his inside breast pocket. The two dark-suited men lead them into the church and locked the door behind them. Then they walked up to the altar. With the altar cloth and crucifix in place, it didn't look any different to what it had before but when Taylor and Stubbs lifted off the cloth it was clear the top slab was a newly carved piece of stone.

The rear stone of the tomb was removed exactly as Simon and Tim had done and then, equipped with torches provided by the two men, the party rolled into the tomb and descended the steps to the oak door. Taylor produced the key and they pulled the door open. The six walked down the remaining steps into the room containing Guy de Bryan's stone tomb, the three wall hangings and the altar at the far end of the room.

As they gazed around the room, Tim stepped forward to the wall hanging behind the altar. He put his hand up to lift back the edge of the heavy cloth when Taylor reached out and grabbed his arm. "Please be careful Mr Woodruff" he cautioned. "Are you and the rest of your party absolutely certain you want to go ahead with this?" Tim turned towards the rest of the group with an enquiring look. One by one, they all nodded. "Very well" said Taylor and taking the bottom corner of the wall hanging he lifted it upwards and to one side, placing a loop attached to the corner of the fabric onto a hook in the wall that, it appeared, had been placed for that very purpose.

"I believe this is what you have been searching for." The curtain was, as Tim had guessed, hiding a second room. Everyone stepped forward almost as one, their torches throwing narrow shafts of light into the darkness. Taylor and McLean had arrived prepared with lamps that gave out a broad beam of illumination and they set them at the entrance to the room and turned them on. The result was spectacular.

The room was similar in size to this first room and again had an altar placed centrally against the wall at the far end but whereas the first altar was bare this one bore a magnificent wooden casket measuring some four feet long by two and a half feet wide and two and a half feet high. It was decorated with gold and each end of the lid was adorned with two gold statues of cherubim angels face to face, their wings outstretched towards each other. Leading to the altar on either side of a central aisle were two sets of menorah, the nine lamp Hebrew candle holders. These stood some four feet high and were also made of gold. Behind them, both the side walls of the room were stacked perhaps seven or eight feet high with columns made of thousands upon thousands of gold coins.

They looked at the scene before them in stunned silence. "It's amazing" breathed Vicki to the nods of the others. "Is that really what I think it is?" said Simon to one of the suits. "If you mean the Ark containing the stone tablets God gave to Moses, then yes, it is" answered McLean. Carwyn was incredulous "Good God boys, I thought you two were wasting your time. I was born and raised here but I never even dreamed..." his voice tailed off. Speaking seemed an irrelevance compared to what they were seeing.

Tim went to step up into this second room but Taylor held him back. "I'm sorry Mr Woodruff but I cannot let you go any further" he said. "Why not?" asked Tim. "Is it because it's a sacred place?" The reply was unexpected: "Er no, because it's not safe" Taylor replied. "What do you mean?" the walls look as sound as they are in here?" "If you venture past this point without the proper protective clothing, you will attract a discharge of electricity from the altar sufficient to cause you serious injury or perhaps even kill you." They were astonished. So this is what the legends meant when they talked about the Power of God. That's why only the chosen priests – presumably properly attired – could enter the Holy of Holies.

After what seemed only a matter of minutes, though in reality was nearer 45, Taylor and McLean gently eased them away from the entrance to the Holy of Holies and replaced the veil. They escorted the party back up the stairs into the church, closing and locking the great oak door as they went. The tomb was closed up and the altar cloth and crucifix returned to their usual places.

"Wow! What an amazing find!" said Tim. "This is going to make us and Laugharne famous around the world" Simon, on the other hand guessed what was coming. Taylor said "I'm afraid not, Mr Woodruff." What do you mean?" said Tim "This is the discovery of the Century. The discovery of a lifetime!" "We cannot possibly let any of you reveal what you have seen today or discuss it with anyone" continued Taylor.

Tim looked uncomprehending. Mclean had been in the front of the party heading towards the church door but now he stopped and quietly turned around to face them all. Although he fixed his cold blue eyes on Tim he addressed his remarks to Simon. "Major Kershaw, have you and your colleagues really thought this through? Can you imagine the consequences if the Ark of the Covenant, one of the greatest relics of the Jewish, Christian and Muslim religions, was suddenly discovered in a sleepy little town in West Wales? The place would be choked with worshippers and tourists from all over the world. The local infrastructure would be unable to cope and the actually quite charming countryside for miles around would be destroyed by the pressure for development.

"Far worse than that though, publicising the Ark would make it a target for every power-mad despot, cult leader, religious fundamentalist and crackpot politician on the planet. I can think of at least three countries that would go to war claiming it rightfully belonged to them. And supposing whoever possessed it gave in to demands for it to be subjected to scientific scrutiny? If it really is a means of controlling or influencing the Power of God who would use it and what would they use it for? If, on the other hand it was claimed to be nothing but a pretty box with angels on top what would this do to the world's major religions? Because, despite all its failings, faith has done much more to improve human existence than those societies without belief, without hope. We think it's better to leave it where it is – people should never meet their heroes, Major."

It was a powerful speech and its end was met with silence. "So what do we do now?" it was Tim that spoke first. "Her Majesty's government and the Church in Wales appreciate the work you have done in researching and protecting the heritage of Wales and the United Kingdom of Great Britain. You must have some influential friends otherwise we would never have allowed you to see what have today. However as you have all signed a document promising you will never, ever, disclose what you have witnessed to anyone, I have been authorised to present you with this sword, the ceremonial sword of Guy de Bryan, as a token of our appreciation for your cooperation."

Simon, Vicki, Tim and Carwyn looked in awe at the gold and jewel-encrusted sword glinting in the daylight streaming through the church windows. "Dyfed-Powys Police are expecting that sword to be handed in as evidence in a trial they have coming up shortly" added McLean. "After that you can have it back and whatever you decide to do with it will be up to you." With that he and Taylor unlocked the church door, smiled at the assembled group and in an instant were gone.

About the Author

Glyn Bryan grew up in Laugharne, West Wales where, on reaching the age of 21, he became a burgess of Laugharne Corporation, an organisation that dates back to 1307. He trained as an agricultural surveyor and after a time with the Ministry of Agriculture began working in agricultural PR and Journalism. In 2012 he gave up business writing and became a non-emergency ambulance driver for the Welsh Ambulance Service. He retired from the Service in 2019 to renovate his late parents' cottage in Laugharne. He is married and he and his wife Jo divide their time between their home in South Wales and their cottage in Laugharne. This is Glyn's first ever attempt at writing fiction.

.

Printed in Great Britain
by Amazon